SHADOW
OF THE RIM

*Also by L. P. Holmes
in Large Print:*

Apache Desert
Bloody Saddles
The Distant Vengeance
Flame of Sunset
High Starlight
Night Marshal
The Plunderers
Rustler's Moon
The Savage Hours
Somewhere They Die

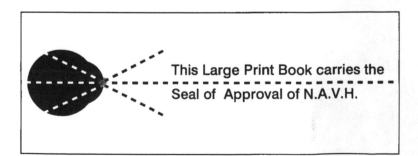

This Large Print Book carries the
Seal of Approval of N.A.V.H.

SHADOW
OF THE RIM

L. P. Holmes

WHEELER
PUBLISHING

Published in 2003 by arrangement with Golden West Literary Agency.

Wheeler Large Print Western Series.

The text of this Large Print edition is unabridged.
Other aspects of the book may vary from the original edition.

Set in 16 pt. Plantin by Ramona A. Watson.

Printed in the United States on permanent paper.

Library of Congress Cataloging-in-Publication Data

Holmes, L. P. (Llewellyn Perry), 1895–
    Shadow of the rim / L.P. Holmes.
      p. cm.
    ISBN 1-58724-472-1 (lg. print : sc : alk. paper)
    1. Inheritance and succession — Fiction.   2. Large type
books. I. Title.
PS3515.O4448S53 2003
 813'.52—dc21
                                                  2003052515

SHADOW
OF THE RIM

As the Founder/CEO of NAVH, the only national health agency solely devoted to those who, although not totally blind, have an eye disease which could lead to serious visual impairment, I am pleased to recognize Thorndike Press★ as one of the leading publishers in the large print field.

Founded in 1954 in San Francisco to prepare large print textbooks for partially seeing children, NAVH became the pioneer and standard setting agency in the preparation of large type.

Today, those publishers who meet our standards carry the prestigious "Seal of Approval" indicating high quality large print. We are delighted that Thorndike Press is one of the publishers whose titles meet these standards. We are also pleased to recognize the significant contribution Thorndike Press is making in this important and growing field.

Lorraine H. Marchi, L.H.D.
Founder/CEO
NAVH

★ Thorndike Press encompasses the following imprints: Thorndike, Wheeler, Walker and Large Print Press.

CHAPTER I

From the doorway of his office in the basement corner of the courthouse, Town Marshal Dan Larkin watched the Iron Mountain stage cross the crest of the Humboldt Rim through a vivid flare of exploding sunset fire, then dip into the steadily deepening tide of smoke-blue early twilight shadow that was beginning to blanket the town.

Dropping down this eastern face of the rim, the switchback road was rough, narrow and steeply crooked, so now, echoing ahead of the stage, came evidence of its nearing approach: grind and scrape of iron-shod wheels on rocky roadbed, dry, squeaking complaint of hard-used hickory brake blocks, together with the clatter of scrambling equine hoofs.

Out of the office depths behind Larkin rose some thinly anxious words. "By what I hear, Dan, that could be the stage. Anybody in sight besides Bill Weeks?"

Ever laconic, the marshal gave a reply that was bluntly so. "Somebody. Not Julie Christiansen, though. If she's with Bill Weeks, she's riding inside."

From the office, Shep Riley voiced further discouraged complaint. "Be just my luck if she ain't even heading home like she was supposed to. And when a man's luck stays bad it can turn him desperate, like I'm gettin' now. If it was just Turk Roderick alone, I'd take my gun and call him out. But the way he plays his cards, it would be me against the whole damn Rolling C outfit, where I'd have no chance at all. I've been hangin' on to the hope that Julie would get home, and if she is on that stage, ridin' inside, maybe a talk with her would pull Roderick off my back. What do you think, Dan?"

Dan Larkin shrugged. He was a grizzled, still-faced man, turned taciturn and aloof by the many mean, tough years he'd carried his badge of authority through a thousand lonely law watches; out of which he had acquired a considerable fund of knowledge regarding people of many kinds, together with their varied, self-centered motives. So, while shrugging a second time, he answered in a gruff growl.

"Wouldn't have any idea at all how Julie's thoughts would be running. She's been gone right on five months. Stands to reason she wouldn't stay away that long without putting considerable faith and trust in Turk Roderick's judgement and the way he looks after Rolling C affairs."

"But Roderick — damn him, he's sure to lie!" Shep Riley's plaint was as thin and reedy as he himself.

"That," conceded Larkin, "could very well

be. Turk was ever one to speak for his own advantage."

"Then you're takin' my word against his?"

"Let's say I'm giving you the benefit of the doubt," corrected Larkin. "Otherwise, I'd have long since booted you out of here and let Roderick and the Rolling C crowd have you."

"I'm not wantin' to cause you any extra trouble," Shep Riley mumbled. "Was my horse handy, I'd make a break and ride for it!"

Dan Larkin cleared an impatient throat. "Talk sense, man — talk sense! I could get your horse for you. See you safe to the edge of town, too. Past that you'd be on your own, and Roderick sure to have you run down and full of lead inside the first short mile. Thing for you to do is lay quiet right here and hope Julie Christiansen is heading home, and maybe will see your side of the deal."

"Providing Turk Roderick will let me talk to her," brooded Shep Riley doubtfully. "I've heard it said that Turk Roderick has more and more been acting like he already owned Rolling C. Owned Julie Christiansen, too. Where is he now?"

"Holding down Wash Butterfield's store steps. Ike Britt is prowling the edges, with the rest of Rolling C just loafing around handy. But quit your fretting. While you're in my custody, in this office, then nobody lays a hand on you without my permission. And should Julie be on the stage, I'll have a talk with her and do the best I can for you."

So saying, Dan Larkin moved into the street and went along it at a measured, steady pace. In the deepening dusk the stage came on across the sagebrush-felted flats between town and the base of the rim, and now rolled through a tunnel of warm gloom under the cottonwoods to haul up at Butterfield's store, one member of the weary team sneezing its relief at this finish of a long run.

Arrival of the Iron Mountain stage was ever a big moment of the day in Humboldt City, being the lone touch of the town with the outside world. So now, all along the street there came a stirring. Cattlehands' high bootheels struck up hollow echoes on board sidewalks and the dragging jangle of spur chains was only partially muffled in the street's dust. Murmured comment by someone brought an answering laugh. From the single eye of early lamplight that spilled through the open door of his store, Wash Butterfield's call rose.

"Heavy mail, Bill?"

"Just the usual." Bill Weeks pulled the mail sack from under the seat and gave it a toss. "Catch!"

Riding the stage box beside the driver, Orde Fraser stretched his arms and shook the dust of travel from a pair of square and solid shoulders. At Iron Mountain he had piled his frugal gear on the stage top and now, preparing to unload it, he paused briefly to wonder how the other passenger of the stage, the one riding inside, was making it.

Remembering her as she stepped off the train at Iron Mountain in her modest blue traveling suit, he thought she had made a slim and, for some reason, lonely figure in a strange, vague way. Also a pretty one, and haughty. For when her first glance met Fraser's quietly admiring one, the chill in her eyes would have frozen a wooden Indian. Yet later, as she hesitated at the high step of the stage and Fraser, tipping his hat, had offered an aiding hand for the lift, she at first went quite still before showing the glimmer of a small, sweet smile as she accepted his help and went lightly up with a soft word of thanks. Recalling these good moments as he rode had helped kill the monotony of hot, dusty miles for Orde Fraser.

Beginning to unload his gear, Fraser lowered his sacked saddle to arm's length before dropping it into the street. After that, with saddle-bags yoked over one shoulder and his scabbarded rifle clasped under an arm, he let himself down. Beside him, the door of the stage swung open and the rustle of skirts sounded. Fraser looked up and offered his free hand.

"This makes it just right. It was my pleasure to help you up, and now my privilege to help you down."

Answer came, but not from the girl. Instead it was a hard, burly shoulder driving into him from the side, together with roughly belligerent words.

11

"Get the hell out of the way, you!"

Knocked off balance by the impact, Orde Fraser spun around, tripped over the sacked saddle at his feet, and went down full-length in the warm dust of the street, held there for a moment by sheer, stunned surprise. Then, seething, he came up and drove in headlong. It was his turn to use a smashing shoulder, followed by a vengeful fist that landed solidly. He missed with a second swing but got home with a third try, driving a man's blurted curse back into his teeth. But the fellow before Fraser was a strong one and came back to meet him, chest to chest. Fraser took a couple of clubbing fists to the face before getting home with another solid smash that sent his man reeling.

Out of the watching dusk came a quick call. "A little trouble maybe, Turk? He giving you a little trouble? Be right with you. . . ."

They came swarming, several of them. For a time Fraser held his own. But sheer weight of numbers drove him back, put him down again. Then boots began thudding into him, so he wrapped his head in his arms and tried to roll free. From somewhere up above sounded feminine cries of protest. But the next several moments became increasingly rugged until the voice of authority eased the pressure.

"Big plenty of this, Roderick — call them off!"

Retort was defiant, thick-toned. "Keep out of it, Larkin. None of your mix!"

The voice of authority turned bleak. "I said — call them off — now! Before somebody gets really hurt — in particular — you. . . ."

That did it. They gave back reluctantly, like a pack of surly dogs whipped off a quarry.

Above Orde Fraser loomed the high bulk of the stage. Close beside him hoofs trampled and chain traces jangled as Bill Weeks, mumbling startled curses, fought to quiet his uneasy team. Fraser's reaching, blindly searching hand found the rim of a wheel that was rocking back and forth. Clinging to it and using it for leverage he hauled himself erect, bracing himself on spread feet while scrubbing a free hand across his punished face. Once he was fairly steady, he gave out his hard, bitter challenge.

"Now we'll see about this little business! Suppose you feed those brave buckos to me, one at a time? That's it, one at a time! I'll enjoy it that way, but they won't. I promise you — they won't!"

A restraining hand gripped his arm and words fell soothingly. "Easy does it, friend. Argument's over. What started it?"

Again Fraser scrubbed a hand across his face, as though to clear his eyes. His answer was tight. "I'm about to offer a young lady a hand down from the stage, when this bucko charged into me like he owned the world and was set to throw me off it. When he found he wasn't man enough to handle that little chore, a flock of real brave ones moved in to help him. Me, I'd admire to have that fellow all to myself for about five minutes. I surely would!"

The hand on his arm stayed firm. "That deal's been played. Best leave it so. Maybe there's something else I can do for you?"

Orde Fraser held quiet for a time, fighting back the raw, wicked anger that rioted through him. Gradually his thinking steadied, so presently he shook himself and drew a deep, relaxing breath.

"Let's say you're right. And you might show me where I can store some of my gear for the night?"

"I'll do better than that," came Dan Larkin's word. "I'll help you pack it there."

Between them they gathered up saddle, saddlebags, rifle and Fraser's hat. On all sides men gave back, some in silence, some still surly and growling. The night was thick with hostility but no further interference was offered as Fraser and his guide went along under the trees to a building that reared high, two-storied shoulders against the evening sky. They turned in at a basement door. A match made its small, bursting flare and then a lamp spread a more generous glow. A chair in a far corner held the hunched figure of a man who stirred uneasily when touched by Fraser's curious glance.

The man with the match said, "Dan Larkin, here. Town Marshal. You? . . ."

"Fraser — Orde Fraser. And obliged mightily for your help. I was in the middle of a damn

14

tough ride until you stepped in to call off the dogs. Incidentally, who was that high and mighty bucko I tangled with?"

"Turk Roderick. Big man of the Rolling C outfit. Out to get bigger and not too particular how he does it." The marshal made grave and searching appraisal of Fraser before adding, "This part of the world is a long way from the rest of it. And staging in with just your saddle gear and a Winchester suggests you're aiming to stay awhile?"

"Awhile," Fraser said, nodding. "There's a hotel?"

"Down street on this side. Anything more?"

"Like to leave my saddle and rifle with you overnight."

"Of course. No handgun?"

Fraser indicated his saddlebags. "In there."

Again the marshal studied him. "Ordinarily, I'd say leave it there. But the way things have shaped up, I won't insist. For the rest, Nell Viney runs a quiet, first-class hotel. Food's first-class, too."

"Sounds just right. I can go along?"

"Sure. A final word. Should you meet with Turk Roderick again, don't press your luck. Man to man, you probably could handle him. But just about always he has some of the Rolling C crew around handy. By and large a rough, tough outfit. And they travel close-herded!"

"As I found out," Orde Fraser admitted ruefully. He shouldered his saddlebags and moved to the door, pausing there. "Strictly none of my business of course, but the this and that of affairs so far has left me a mite curious. The young lady on the stage?"

"Miss Julia Christiansen. Owner of the Rolling C outfit. Owner of the town bank, too."

Considering this word, Orde Fraser frowned thoughtfully. He made as if to speak further, then reconsidered, shaking his head. He stepped into the darkening street.

Shep Riley came out of his corner chair eagerly. "So Julie was on the stage! You speak to her about me?"

"Had no chance, what with the ruckus that took place," Larkin said. "And after the long haul in from Iron Mountain, I doubt she'll head on out to ranch headquarters tonight. I'll try to see her later and let you know about things when I bring your supper."

"That new feller," Shep pressed. "Who is he and what's he doin' here?"

Dan Larkin grunted impatiently. "You heard what he had to say. Past that, I don't know any more about him than you do. Except that he can damn well handle himself in a brawl."

"The row that went on down the street — that was him tangling with Turk Roderick?"

"Just so. And with Roderick beginning to take a currying until Ike Britt and the others moved in."

Shep Riley complained bitterly, "That's

Rolling C for you. The way they fight — always in a crowd. Me, I sure would have enjoyed seeing Turk Roderick get belted a couple of good ones!"

Just the faintest hint of a smile traced its way across Dan Larkin's face. "Sort of enjoyed that part, myself."

Like the courthouse, Nell Viney's Rimview Hotel was two-storied. A deep, full-length porch held a scatter of well-used chairs, all empty at the moment. The beckoning radiance of lamplight guided Orde Fraser into a small lobby. A flight of stairs slanted up the far inner wall and a register desk occupied one corner. From behind this, an angular, red-haired, pleasant-faced woman made a shrewd appraisal of Fraser before smiling and offering an amused greeting.

"I just heard that some stranger had considerably mussed up Turk Roderick. By the signs, you must be the one who did it. And if it's lodging you're after, I've a mind to offer it free."

Fraser smiled crookedly. "Should that happen, I've reason to feel that I'd earned it. Because the go-round was anything but one-sided, and I know I've been over the jumps. I do want a room. Supper, too. And likely more of the same for the next several days."

He signed the register with vigorous strokes. The redhead reversed the book and murmured as she read.

"Orde Fraser. From Tuscarora?"

"Thereabouts," Fraser said, nodding. "Nearest post office to my last campfire."

Nell Viney sighed enviously. "Another lucky drifter, eh? Not a thing on your mind while chasing your shadow down the next trail."

"Nothing near that simple," Fraser protested. "And not all roses along such trails — just plenty of rough spots."

Nell Viney laughed. "Number two. First door on the right at the head of the stairs. Should you want to clean up, you'll find the water cold. But I'll have some hot brought up if you'd like it so. Might help the sore spots, too."

Fraser shouldered his saddlebags. "Cold will do fine."

He climbed the stairs, turned into the room, bumped into a chair and stacked his gear on it. Scratching a match alight, he located a bracket wall lamp and by the light of this surveyed the room. A plain pine-wood bureau held a wash-basin and water pitcher. A spotlessly clean towel hung on a wall peg. There was a shard of mirror above the bureau and in this he had a look at himself, running carefully exploring fingers over the bruised spots on his cheeks. Whiskers rasped under his touch, so he opened his saddlebags and got out his soap and razor, now wishing that he'd taken Nell Viney up on the offer of hot water. As it was, cold would have to do.

He stripped to the waist, his boot-punished

torso gleaming white in contrast to the deep, weathered tan of his face and neck. At twenty-eight he was a supple, solidly built man with a wide chest and shoulders from which a swell of muscle tapered down to a saddle man's nipped-in flanks. His thick hair was ruddy bronze, his eyes a shade of gray just off blue. His normally level mouth was pulled a trifle out of shape by the marks of conflict. High on his left cheek an ancient scar traced its faint, streaked way.

He soaped his face and began to shave, swearing mildly at the razor's pull. But when it was done and he'd had a good wash, he felt better. Likewise hungry. He got a clean shirt from his saddlebags, shook out the worst of the wrinkles, and donned it. He combed his hair with his fingers and decided he'd get by for supper.

He rummaged through his saddlebags again. His Colt, holstered and wrapped in the cartridge belt, he left where it was, while pocketing a fresh sack of Durham tobacco. He hesitated slightly before sliding a legal-sized envelope inside his shirt, then moved to the room's lone window and looked out across the town's rooftops while reflecting on the vagaries of fortune that could beset a man.

Short weeks ago he'd been far back on the Stony River range, ramrodding Tom Kenshaw's K Bar outfit. Now he was here, getting first look at a new stretch of country that held for him an inheritance as unexpected as it was difficult to believe. The end result of a distant and near-forgotten family tie, plus lengthy court litigation he'd neither taken part in nor been overly concerned about. Yet, here he was. And out there somewhere lay the inheritance, if he was man enough to claim it. . . .

Full dark had now settled in. Directly ahead, beyond the run of outlying sagebrush flats, the Humboldt Rim bulked massively and, above its black crest, evening's first stars scattered their cautious glitter. On the street below, reflected lamplight splashed the cooling dust with pools of thin, amber glow. In the leafy sanctuary of the town's cottonwood trees, sparrows chirped sleepily. There also, early on a nocturnal hunt, a screech owl whimpered fretfully. At town's far edge a dog's ragged barking beat up a single harsh note across the peace of evening. Now, abruptly, on the hotel porch below, an iron triangle beat up a resonant supper call.

By the time Orde Fraser got downstairs, several of Nell Viney's regulars were moving through the lobby toward the dining room. One of the early arrivals was Marshal Dan Larkin, and Fraser fell into step with him.

"Another small favor, maybe?"

Larkin's glance was questioning. "Such as? . . ."

"The young lady who was on the stage," Fraser said carefully. "You named her as Julie Christiansen, owner of the Rolling C outfit. If she is in the dining room, you might introduce me."

Dan Larkin's step slowed and his look turned cold and narrow. Quick to understand, Fraser's further explanation was brief. "Strictly a matter of business, you understand. Nothing more."

Still tough and wary, Larkin gave a response that was a blunt growl. "What kind of business? If it's a riding job, you're wasting your time. All the hiring and firing at Rolling C is done by that same rough character you tangled with, Turk Roderick."

Fraser shook his head. "No job at all. But a question of possession."

"So-o! That makes me ask — possession of what?"

"The Milliken Indian grant."

Caught with a deeper interest, Dan Larkin came to a complete halt. "First time I've heard it called that since Yance Milliken died. Hereabouts it's known as the Shoshone Lake range and considered as public domain. Yance's father, old Silas Milliken, so I've heard it said, never did come up with clear proof of his claim of getting it through that Indian grant, so where does any question of ownership come into the picture?"

"Simple enough," Fraser said tersely. "Aware that his father's claim was under question, Yance set out to prove the old man right. He put the matter in the courts. Unfortunately, Yance died before the litigation was fully settled. However, the record now stands cleared, and title of old Silas Milliken's grant adjudged and binding. Back taxes have been paid. So that range is not public domain, and the only brand legally working it is the Milliken Double Diamond."

Dan Larkin scowled at the floor, scuffing an open palm across his chin. Presently his glance lifted. "Say all that is so. Where do you fit in? You speaking for the Milliken estate?"

"No — for myself."

"How — for yourself?"

"Happens I'm a far-out relative of Yance Milliken on my mother's side of the family. So far out, in fact, I never tried to follow it up or expect anything from it, either. But just recently a bank in Winnemucca that represented the Milliken interests ran me down and told me that as the lone survivor of the Milliken clan, the Milliken range was mine by inheritance. So I'm here to claim it."

Dan Larkin exclaimed softly. "Be damned! You can back up all this with proof?"

"Beyond question."

Larkin turned deeply serious. "Then you got big trouble ahead, boy!"

"That's the reason I want a talk with Miss Christiansen," Orde Fraser said. "An agreement with her could head off any trouble."

"Maybe yes, maybe no," Larkin said. "Rolling C isn't the only outfit you'll have to argue with. Right now Hollis Ward has cattle feeding on Shoshone Lake grass. So has Starr Jennette. And the little one-man outfits like Poe

22

Darby, Andy Quider and Shep Riley. Nobody's going to let go easy of that chunk of range. I'm damn sure Rolling C won't — not while Turk Roderick is ramrodding it."

Fraser shrugged. "Easy or hard, they'll have to move out. I want no trouble with anyone, but I intend to claim what is mine. That fellow Roderick may be riding boss of Rolling C, but it is Miss Christiansen who owns the spread, so it should be her word that counts."

"All right," nodded Larkin, "I concede that point. But don't count too heavy on Julie seeing things your way. She's one hell of a fine girl, but not Buckley Christiansen's daughter for nothing. There never was a tougher old blister than Buck Christiansen when he got his neck bowed. He and Si Milliken were a pair of feisty old devils who hated each other clear across the boards. So it's quite possible you'll meet up with some of Buck Christiansen's stubborn toughness in his lovely daughter. But come along. If Julie's inside, I'll give you the knockdown and wish you luck. You'll damn well need it!"

CHAPTER II

The dining room held one large center table and several smaller ones ranked against the walls. At one of these smaller ones, Julie Christiansen sat. Across from her was a yellow-headed man with heavy, down-sloping shoulders. Observing this, Dan Larkin exclaimed in soft words to Orde Fraser.

"Uh — oh! Friend, this won't be easy. That's Turk Roderick with her, and by the look of things, she's been working Roderick over with the spurs!"

Popular with town regulars, the center table held several of them, who had friendly nods for Dan Larkin and a guarded, speculative appraisal of Orde Fraser. Intent on what she was saying to her companion, Julie Christiansen was unaware of the approach of Fraser and the marshal until they stopped beside her. Then her head came up, quick and imperious.

"Yes? . . ."

Turk Roderick also looked up. His reaction was an eruptive, throaty growl. He pushed back his chair and started to rise, a move quickly forestalled by the weight of Dan Larkin's hand and blunt, terse order.

"Stay put, Turk! Let's all act civilized for a

change." Then swiftly and in milder tone he added, "Miss Julie — meet Orde Fraser. He'd like a business talk with you."

The answer was hesitant and a trifle defensive. "I can't imagine why. If it is about a riding job at Rolling C, the person to talk to would be Mr. Roderick, my foreman."

Orde Fraser shook his head. "Not a riding job, Miss Christiansen. Something much more important, to which I think you'll agree if you'll allow me to explain."

Like his glance, his words were respectful, but direct. Under the impact of them, a touch of color stole across the smooth curve of her cheek. Parted in the middle, her hair swept back in thick folds, capping her head with a rich, dark-honey luxury. She had changed from her traveling outfit into a simple house dress that made her seem younger and more girlish. Here, decided Orde Fraser, was a young woman who was decidedly attractive by any standard, though just now made distant and hostile by some resolute inner compulsion.

"I'm afraid," she said flatly, "I'd have to know more about this important business."

"Fair enough," Fraser agreed. "Would you consider my proven ownership of the old Milliken Indian grant a matter of sufficient importance?"

Her slim shoulders stiffened and she came forward in her chair, staring up at him. Turk Roderick's growl erupted again and this time the weight of Marshal Dan Larkin's hand was not enough to keep the Rolling C foreman in his chair. He surged erect, his voice heavy and carrying.

"There is no such thing as a Milliken Indian grant. That country is the Shoshone Lake range and free government land."

As did Orde Fraser himself, this fellow Turk Roderick carried strong marks of the brief brawl that had taken place when the stage from Iron Mountain hauled up in front of Wash Butterfield's store. His lips had thickened into a pout, and bruises lay dark under each eye. His corn-yellow hair was shaggy and rumpled. Florid of face, heavy of feature, he carried the blaze of a ruthless truculence in a pair of rock-hard eyes, and there was a challenging swing of his heavy shoulders to emphasize his words. The carrying weight of his tone brought a turning of heads about the room, a reaction that caused the girl to stir uneasily. Her words were crisp with authority as she spoke to quiet him.

"That will do, Turk! I'll handle this."

With just the barest edge of hesitation she looked up at Orde Fraser again and conceded the point.

"Very well. I'll see you in the hotel parlor half an hour from now."

To Orde Fraser there came again the thought that here was a young person plagued with a lonely uncertainty. He tipped his head and spoke gently. "Thank you. I'll be there."

He moved on to a vacant table, drawing Dan Larkin with him. "A favor for a favor," he said. "I'm buying your supper."

Larkin settled into his chair with a sigh of relief. "Got by better than I hoped. You handled your part just right. Julie surprised me. Surprised Turk Roderick, too — putting the check on him the way she did. Could be that while on her trip outside, she's figured a new slant on things."

"Such as? . . ." Fraser prompted.

Dan Larkin shook a gruff head. "Ain't saying. This run of country has its faults, but gossiping over the personal affairs of other folks ain't one of them."

A pair of sturdy, quick-moving Indian girls did most of the waiting on table, but it was Nell Viney herself who put food in front of Fraser and the marshal, together with a soberness of manner and some direct words for Larkin.

"Dan, I understand Starr Jennette just hit town and is over at Pete Eagle's Ten High Bar. You think he somehow got word that Julie Christiansen was arriving home tonight?"

"Wouldn't know, couldn't guess, and ain't about to try," Larkin said. "Like I just told Fraser here, the personal affairs of other folks is their business entirely, and none of mine. None of yours either, Nellie."

Nell Viney tossed a red head. "Bosh! I've known Julie Christiansen since she had to

27

climb a corral fence to get high enough to straddle a horse. Fact is, I've more than half-way raised her. And no matter what that pig-headed old tarantula, Buckley Christiansen, ever said or tried to arrange, I'm not about to see the girl pestered by Starr Jennette or anyone else. He comes prowling around my hotel, I'll run him off with a gun — which he darn well knows!"

Dan Larkin lifted a placating hand. "Now — now, Nellie — get off the warpath. Most likely you're borrowing trouble that will never show. Only interest I got in Starr Jennette just now is to keep him from stirring up a ruckus of some sort with the Rolling C outfit." He looked across at Orde Fraser. "Hope you won't mind if I hurry through my grub and get back on the street?"

"Make the time your own," Fraser told him. "Once more, thanks for everything. Should I ever come in handy in any way, just say the word."

Larkin grunted. "Best way you can help to-night is have your little talk with Julie Christiansen and stay off the street."

Fraser smiled faintly. "Nothing like that. I expect to travel that street quite often, so I don't begin by staying off it."

"Always like that," Larkin grumbled. "Stubborn, stiff-necked people!" He called after Nell Viney, who was about to move away, "Save a meal, Nellie — for a feller I got in my office. I'll be in for it later."

Saying which, the marshal was quickly through and gone. Orde Fraser ate hungrily, but leisurely. Half an hour, Julie Christiansen had said. Which gave him plenty of time. Shortly after Dan Larkin left, Turk Roderick and the girl came away from their chairs. Passing the center table and the wondering but cautious glances lifting from it, Julie Christiansen held her head high and her shoulders very straight. As though, Fraser thought, she were challenging and defying public opinion on some issue.

He was pondering over this as he finished his meal. He spun up a cigarette and dawdled a bit over his final cup of coffee. After which, he left the dining room and crossed the lobby to the door of the hotel parlor.

Julie Christiansen was alone, huddled on a worn, high-backed sofa, elbow on knee, chin couched in the palm of her hand. There was a lost, lonely look about her. As though this thought of Fraser's had been transmitted to her, she straightened quickly, and the glance she showed him was as cold and distant as that first chill one she'd given him back at Iron Mountain.

There was a chair to match the sofa, and Fraser skidded this around to face her. "All right if I sit down?"

Her nod was slight, the shield of chill not lowering in the slightest. "You'll be brief, please! I'm very tired."

"Wouldn't wonder a bit at that," Fraser agreed cheerfully. "The stage haul in from Iron Mountain would tire anybody. So — to business. It happens that I have inherited the old Milliken Indian grant range, known hereabouts as the Shoshone Lake range. Right now, several outfits — yours among them — are running cattle on that range, claiming it to be open public land. That is an empty claim. The range is mine and all brands other than my own must move off it. I'm hoping this can be arranged amicably, as I want to live at peace with my neighbors. As owner of the largest outfit concerned, you would help matters greatly if you'd see matters that way."

Denial was quick and emphatic. "To the contrary! Shoshone Lake has always been open range. I know the Millikens claimed differently, but my father never recognized that claim as legitimate and neither do I!"

Orde Fraser produced the legal envelope he'd tucked inside his shirt, tapping it with a finger. "It's in here — all of it. Legal proof of my claim. Care to examine it?"

Again that quick, denying shake of the head. "Such things can be contrived — and are! Also, men can, and do, lie!" She got to her feet, slim and straight. "The Rolling C cattle now on Shoshone Lake range will stay there! Does that answer you?"

Fraser rose to face her. "It is an answer," he said soberly. "But neither the right one nor the one I had hoped for. Also, it clouds the future with the shadow of certain trouble. No matter! I will take possession of what is legally mine and, by whatever means necessary, clear it of all brands but my own!"

He was a lean, solid man, rugged all the way through and built to endure. And though his glance was level and stern, presently the glimmer of a smile showed.

"Believe me, Miss Christiansen, I do not enjoy bullying you in this manner. So I am hoping you'll come around to a more open mind on our problem. For some reason you seem to have little trust of the world or of the people in it. I would hate to be responsible for that feeling and certainly have no desire to make it worse."

Still coldly defiant, she moved to the door, pausing there for a final unrelenting retort, "Your reference to my personal affairs is uncalled for. And my feelings about the Shoshone Lake range will never change!"

"Never," countered Orde Fraser gently, "is a long, long time!"

Saying nothing more, she whisked herself away. Sorting out his thoughts, Fraser eyed the empty doorway.

"There," he murmured presently, "goes a young lady running scared of something or someone. . . ."

He was still speculating on it when he returned to his room. At the supper table Dan

Larkin and Nell Viney had traded opinions on Julie Christiansen and her affairs. And though the marshal had deftly sidestepped any direct reference one way or the other, Nell Viney had expressed herself openly and vigorously in defending the girl. She had also brought in the name of one Starr Jennette with a strong show of hostility toward the owner of it. Which suggested that some sort of complication, romantic or otherwise, could exist there.

Restless with his thoughts, Fraser donned his hat and shrugged into his old, use-faded jumper. He eyed his saddlebags with some indecision. Earlier, the marshal had cautioned him about wearing a gun in town. And though he had his bruises to remind him that where he was concerned, this Humboldt Rim country was hardly a friendly one, at the moment he could see no good reason for strapping on a weapon. This decided on, he swept a cupped hand past the lamp's chimney top and, as the flame flickered out, moved on into the hall. The scurry of light, ascending footsteps could be heard now on the stairs and then it was Julie Christiansen who faced him. She was held with a startled glance before she slipped by, turning into another room farther along.

Dimly lighted by a pair of wall bracket lamps, the hallway ran the full length of the building to a closed door at the far end. Ever one mindful of the full limits and layout of his surroundings, Fraser went quietly along to that rear door, opened it, and looked at a down flight of stairs reaching to the dark earth below, thus furnishing a second means of entrance or exit to the hotel. He closed the door, retraced his steps and dropped down to the lobby where Nell Viney was wielding a vigorous broom. She paused to eye him.

"In suggesting that you keep off the street tonight, Dan Larkin meant well, you know."

"No question," Fraser agreed. "But I long ago got over being afraid of the dark."

Nell Viney laughed softly. "I could have told Dan that. How was the room — and the supper?"

"None better anywhere," he assured her, going on out into the night.

Overhead the great arch of the sky was all awash with massed star glitter, and against this the rim towered, grim and black. As he moved toward Butterfield's store, it was Fraser's first thought that but for several saddle mounts scattered here and there along the town's hitch rails the street was empty. Now, beyond one of the rails, saloon doors winnowed, letting out a flare of light and a pair of swift-moving figures quickly lost in night's solid gloom under the trees. It would have been a thing of little note except for a suggestion of furtiveness. Fraser's awareness of his surroundings sharpened.

Now, from another quarter, came a stir of movement and the drone of guarded voices. Suddenly the street proved itself far from empty. Men clung to the thick shadows and the dark was charged with tension and a sense of breathless waiting.

Orde Fraser thought of the gun he'd left in his room, half of a mind to go back after it. Then the saloon doors winnowed again, letting out the solid, reassuring figure of Dan Larkin who, after a brief survey of the night, headed up and across toward the hotel. Fraser shrugged aside his moment of uneasiness and climbed the step of Butterfield's store. This was Dan Larkin's town and with him cruising it, the night should be quiet enough.

Wash Butterfield stood behind a cluttered counter. Gangling in stature, bald-headed and long of face, his glance was shrewd and speculative before he nodded and uttered brief greeting.

"Evening!"

Orde Fraser identified himself. "From time to time there could be mail for me. If I'm not immediately on hand, will you hold it?"

"Once it gets here, it will stay here," Butterfield told him. "This is big country and folks living far out don't hit town too often. I've held mail for some as long as six months, so any that comes for you will be here when you call."

"Obliged," Fraser said.

He was turning away when the cry lifted, high and wild, full of fear and protest, frantic with desperation. It came from up by the courthouse, a man's yell of mortal terror.

"No, Britt — no! You can't do this to me! You got no cause, no real cause. No, I tell you — for God's sake . . . no!"

Terrifying as it was in its lifting abruptness, the cry broke off just as suddenly. And now a new and different yell lifted, shrill with mockery and malign triumph. Close on the heels of this came the bursting rush of hoofs speeding along the street.

Wash Butterfield's reaction was harsh exclamation. "Knew it! Knew something was going to break. There's been the smell of some kind of hell brewing all afternoon!"

With these words he ran out on the porch, Orde Fraser moving with him. The rush of speeding hoofs became a nearing thing. Charging past through the street's shuttered pattern of light and dark, the rider was caught fully in the flare of light from the store's wide doorway. He was a stocky one, this rider, low-crouched and half-turned in his saddle so he could look back at what was dragging at the far end of the rope stretched tautly from his saddle horn. What he was looking at was something that rolled and tumbled and twisted with arms and legs whipping wildly, and by this time, limply.

From a pocket of gloom a second whoop of mockery lifted, followed by three hard, smashing gun reports; and lead raked the dust about the dragging figure. Came a breath-short

35

pause before the gun boomed twice more and a pair of slugs crunched into the front of the store, whipping past Orde Fraser so closely it seemed he felt the hot breath of them.

Instantly moving, Fraser's quick, long strides whirled him back into the store. Wash Butterfield scrambling behind him and sputtering outraged anger.

"You see that? Ike Britt dragging a man! And that fool with the gun — he came near hitting us. Almost like he was shooting at us on purpose!"

"Which he was!" charged Fraser savagely. "At me in particular. Those last two shots were nowhere near the poor devil on the end of the rope — they were at me! And if that's the way this damned range wants to play the game, that's the way it is going to be played!"

"Ain't the range," defended Butterfield, still sputtering his wrath. "No, not the range. Just some of the people traveling across it. Like that fellow Turk Roderick and the mongrel crew he's gathered out at Rolling C. Right now Roderick is running wild and Julie Christiansen will never be able to handle him!"

"Britt," rapped Fraser. "You named the rider as Britt?"

"Ike Britt," affirmed Butterfield. "A bad one — a real bad one. Turk Roderick's pet mad dog. Anything Roderick tells him to do — that's it."

Wolf-restless, Orde Fraser moved to the door.

"I'll remember Ike Britt. Likewise his boss, Mister Roderick. And in particular the damned sneak who threw those shots! . . ."

Outside, the street was charged with wild activity. Men were rushing around, calling back and forth. One voice lifted above all the others, charged with a bitter outrage. The voice of Marshal Dan Larkin.

Fraser had his own brief but careful look at things before dodging out and running along the porch to its far end, there losing himself in the thick dark beyond. With this sheltering cover he made swift way back to the hotel and up to his room. He touched a match to the bracket lamp and dug into his saddlebags, bringing out his gun and belting it on. Even as he set the belt to its proper tension, the door of his room began to edge guardedly open. Gun half-drawn, he whirled, then went motionless and incredulous. The person who slipped into the room and closed the door behind her was Julie Christiansen!

She was wrapped to the chin in a brightly patterned robe and her feet were in beaded moccasins. Her hair fell in loose, rippling folds over her slim shoulders. Her face was pale, her eyes deep pools of agitated pleading. Stirred by quickened breathing, her words fell softly.

"Please! You must try to understand. Please . . . I'm not here. If anyone calls at your door — I'm not here! You must understand . . . please! . . ."

Sheer amazement held Orde Fraser speech-less. Asked to name the last person on earth likely to enter his room at this hour and in this manner, he would have to name this haughty, hostile, aloof young woman!

Young woman — hell! More like a scared little kid. Yeah — just a scared little kid, running from ghosts or something of the sort.

"All right," he said, finally finding words. "If that's the way you want it, that's the way it is. You're not here. Who would likely think otherwise?"

Before answering, she scurried to the deepest corner of shadow in the room, from there again offering a breathless, half-whispered pleading.

"My being here like — this — it — it's not at all what you might think. And anyone else — they must not know. . . ."

About to speak further, she instead came up on tiptoe, listening intently, then laying a cautioning finger on her lips. So now Orde Fraser listened and heard them — measured steps advancing along the hallway from the rear. It was a broken advance, with several short pauses, at which times the dry creak of doors — cautiously opened and closed — sounded. Whoever was in the hall was checking each room along the way.

Orde Fraser moved closer to his own door, gun loose and ready in his hand. When the approaching steps came even and the door began to edge open, he swung it wide, filling it with a pair of challenging shoulders and a harsh-voiced demand.

"What the hell is this? What's going on here? Who would you be, prowling and opening doors without bothering to knock?"

The man facing him was lithe and swarthy, with dark eyes looking out of an even-featured face. A gun swung at the rider's narrow hips, but the owner made no move toward it. Instead, unperturbed, he eyed the weapon in Fraser's fist.

"You figure it necessary to wave that?"

"What else?" Fraser retorted. "Minutes ago, down on the street, somebody tried twice for me from the dark. I didn't have my gun with me then, but I got it now, and taking no more chances. Again, who might you be?"

"The name," came the even reply, "is Jennette — Starr Jennette. Never having laid eyes on you before, you have to be a stranger." Again the dark-eyed glance touched Fraser's gun. "Also, I didn't throw any lead your way. Had I done so, you wouldn't be here now. As for the rest — sorry to have bothered."

So saying, the speaker turned away and went back along the hall to the outside stairs beyond. Orde Fraser waited until departure was complete before closing his own door and turning to the girl in the corner.

"Is he what you're running from?"

She hesitated before showing a small, fatalistic shrug. "If you put matters that way — yes, he is part of it."

"How did you know he'd be along the hall, looking for you?"

"I saw him from my window. He was circling the hotel to come up the back way."

"Why wouldn't he come in the front way?"

"Nell Viney. He knew he couldn't get by her."

"I didn't see any horns on him — or cloven hooves, either," Fraser commented dryly.

Again she paused as though searching carefully for just the right words. "There could be so many things you do not understand."

"No question about that," Fraser agreed. "But with Nell Viney such a refuge, why didn't you run to her for shelter?"

The girl flushed, looking down at her robe. "I couldn't appear in the lobby like this."

"But you could in the room of a complete stranger?"

Flush became deep, hot color. Answer was subdued. "I — I was desperate. I didn't know where to turn. I had to hide somewhere as I wasn't prepared to face him just yet. Earlier today, you were kind to me, acting the gentleman in offering to help me on and off the stage. So I gambled you'd help me again."

She was confused, frightened, shamed. Again she seemed so young, and Fraser knew a rush of sympathy for her, and spoke accordingly.

"It's over now, and quite all right. It concerns nobody but you and me, and is now safe for you to go back to your own room."

She shook her head. "Presently — but not just yet, please."

She went over to the window and looked down at the street below. Fraser moved up beside her.

"Making certain he's down there?"

Wordless, she nodded. The top of her head came even with his shoulder, and of a sudden her presence, there close beside him, became a warm, disturbing thing. He studied her guardedly and by the tide of color washing up her throat and across her cheeks, knew she was aware of his searching interest. Recalling the forlorn, lonely figure she had made in the hotel parlor earlier, he now offered quiet suggestion.

"I've no idea what you'd be running from, but whatever it is, best face and settle it, one way or the other. Strictly none of my business, of course, but I will say this: There is no profit in running from anything forever."

She started slightly as though once again his spoken thought had meshed with her own silent one. "I know," she conceded soberly. "And I'm fighting to find the necessary nerve to make that decision."

"Probably won't be as difficult as you think," he encouraged. "Nothing ever is, really."

Down on the street a lithe, quick-striding figure moved through light flare and shadow to the saloon and entered there. Beside Fraser the girl gave a little sigh of relief and turned to leave. "You've been very kind and I thank you deeply." Then, caught with a recollected thought, she paused and showed him a direct, shadowed glance.

"I heard what you said about someone shooting at you?"

Fraser nodded. "It happened."

"Any idea who did it, or why?"

"Right now, either way would be a guess," Fraser said. "I was a fat target, up there on the store porch. Could be that the bucko who tried for me will wish he hadn't missed."

A small fierceness fired Julie Christiansen's next words. "This range has always been my home, but there are times when I hate it, and wonder why I ever returned to it!"

"But now perhaps have found the reason why you did?" Fraser suggested.

She considered a moment, looking down at the floor. Then her head came proudly up and the earlier spirit and defiance flared in her glance.

"Yes. Yes — that is so. It is as you say. A person cannot run from legitimate responsibilities and still hope to live at peace with themselves. Also, it seems I wasn't raised to be a quitter!"

"Good girl!" Fraser applauded. "That's the spirit!"

She went to the door and turned, her glance meeting his fairly and steadily. As she spoke there came again the small, sweet smile that softened the lines of her face and turned them lovely.

"It is all so very strange. If I think on it enough I may yet understand fully why and how I instinctively turned to you for refuge. To you — a complete stranger! Yet that is how it was, and in the light of calm reason, hardly makes sense. It is also a fact that you have been very kind and considerate, showing me a respect and generosity I hardly deserve or have the right to expect. For all of it I again thank you so truly, truly. Nor will I forget!"

After that she was swiftly gone.

Alone, Orde Fraser stood for a time, staring at the closed door while turning the entire incident over and over again in his thoughts. It was easy to believe that it had never happened at all — that he had imagined the whole thing. Yet it had been completely real, every moment of it. The faintest breath of a violet fragrance lingered in the room and he shook his head at the sheer wonder of it. . . .

But now came the facts of sterner business to be faced. He put out the light and left the room.

CHAPTER III

Orde Fraser stepped into a street that now lay empty and quiet along its reaches up by the courthouse. At its lower end, however, where stable and freight corrals made their odorous sprawl, all was sound and activity. Several lanterns wove restless patterns of light, and the roll of men's voices laid a heavy, growling note across the night.

Moving warily, Fraser sought the deep shadow at the corner of Butterfield's store, pausing there to test all the currents of the dark. Clear above all voices, made harsh by a bitterly savage anger, rose Marshal Dan Larkin's reply to some questioner.

"Is Shep Riley dead? Hell, yes — of course he is. The poor little devil is all busted up besides having a couple of bullet holes through him. Happened like this. Shep was holed up in my office, under my official protection. I went over to the hotel after some grub for him. That was the chance they've been waiting half a day for, to catch him alone. So they hauled him out of my office, dropped a loop around his neck and dragged him to death, adding some .45 slugs to make sure. A damned rotten, cowardly deal! For which, somebody pays to me — to me, by

44

God! Now give a hand, so we can get him under cover."

The weaving lanterns moved over and into the stable. Presently men began drifting back up town, a number of them cutting over to the Ten High Bar. Then it was Dan Larkin and Wash Butterfield who came along to stop in front of the store in earshot of where Orde Fraser waited and watched and listened. Butterfield was making sober-voiced comment.

"Bad business, Dan. As raw a flouting of public rights and the authority of law as I ever heard of. Nor can I see Ike Britt figuring it out by himself. He had to be following orders."

"Just so!" agreed Larkin, growling. "Whose orders? Had to be Turk Roderick's."

Butterfield nodded. "With Julie Christiansen standing behind Roderick. Which makes the whole affair particularly ugly."

"Haul up, Wash — haul up!" Dan Larkin's rebuke was quick and stern. "No more of that talk. You should know better than to bring that fine girl's name into a mess like this. Hell, man — she just arrived home this evening."

"I know — I know!" Butterfield admitted hurriedly. "Of course she had no direct part in it. I didn't mean it so. But the fact remains that she owns Rolling C and there will be some who will hold her responsible for anything and everything the outfit does, good or bad. Also, there are those who well remember how old Buck Christiansen, through the power of his outfit

45

and his bank, ran this stretch of country pretty much to suit his own ends. People don't forget such things. So there's bound to be plenty of talk about tonight's miserable affair, and not all that talk will be too kind to Julie Christiansen. Regrettable, of course, but still an unfortunate fact."

"No matter," declared Larkin flatly. "Nobody downtalks that girl in front of me and gets away with it. I expect you to take the same stand. And now, if Mister Turk Roderick is still in town, he's due to meet some facts of life — the hard way!"

"Meaning what?" Butterfield asked, a thread of uneasiness behind his words.

"For a start, to find out what it's like to spend some time behind bars!"

Wash Butterfield scrubbed an anxious hand across his chin. "Don't get too far out on a limb, Dan. Whatever else Roderick might be, he is also a proud man. And wherever he is, he won't be alone; but you will be. Understand, I make no defense of the man or of the outfit he bosses. But the fact remains that Rolling C is the big, he-wolf power in this neck of the woods. So, were I you, I'd go a little easy."

Dan Larkin swung restless shoulders. "You call Roderick a proud man. Well, hell! In some ways I'm pretty damn proud myself. Shep Riley was in my office under the protection of my badge. But they hauled him out and killed him — which I don't stand still for. I don't care if

Roderick's alone or has fifty of his kind behind him. This is where he finds out who's running this town!"

So saying, Dan Larkin headed for the Ten High Bar, his step quick and purposeful. Wash Butterfield sighed and turned into his store and began locking up for the night. From the shadow, Orde Fraser watched until the saloon door closed behind Dan Larkin, then crossed and went in after him.

The saloon was crowded and charged with cautious and uneasy talk. Behind the bar, Pete Eagle moved quickly back and forth, his broad, brown cheeks strictly neutral. A full-blooded Shoshone Indian, Pete Eagle had long ago learned the wisdom of steering clear of the affairs of other men and — so far as was possible — of treating them all alike. A chunky, powerful man, he owned a quiet dignity and carried a spark in his level, black-eyed glance that warned would-be troublemakers to beware. On occasion, when it was strictly necessary, he had displayed the ability to back up that warning. In the main, he was well liked and well thought of.

Easing to one side, Orde Fraser put his shoulders against a wall and took quiet measure of the room and the people in it. At the bar, a glass of whiskey in his hand, Turk Roderick was a central figure, flanked on either side by members of his crew. It was, Fraser thought, as though they would show the world a united front.

Over against a far wall, straddling a reversed chair, arms folded across the back of it while watching the play of affairs with an air of cynical unconcern, was the dark-faced rider who had prowled the hotel hallway earlier and named himself as Starr Jennette.

On entering the room, Dan Larkin had made a steady way along the front of the bar to now stand squared in front of Turk Roderick, his words falling bluntly.

"That was murder out there, Roderick — cold-blooded, cowardly murder! And you don't get away with it. Let's have your gun — I'm locking you up!"

"Locking me up?" Roderick stared, an arrogant truculence filming his pale eyes. "I didn't do anything."

"Ike Britt did," retorted Larkin harshly. "A dirty, stupid clod, Ike Britt! One of your pet faithfuls. He does only what you tell him to do. And should he ever show in this town again, I'll shoot him on sight. If you figure on drinking that whiskey, get it done! And come along." He held out his hand. "Your gun!"

Instead of complying, Roderick swung his head, laying a glance right and left. The move carried a meaning which brought his men crowding even closer to him. After which he returned his regard to the marshal, mocking and sardonic.

"You see how it is, Larkin? This outfit rides together. You figure to take me in, you got to

48

take all of us. Think you're up to the chore? I don't!"

From beyond the bar, Pete Eagle tried to show Dan Larkin a slight shake of his head. Pete liked the marshal and respected his integrity and ability, but right now the odds were a little too heavy. Pete's warning was wasted. Dan Larkin's full attention was fixed on this arrogant, sneering fellow in front of him.

A Rolling C rider, openly snickering, making as if he had stumbled, lurched into the marshal. Larkin's reaction was wickedly fast and savage. He grabbed the puncher by the shoulders, spun him around, kicked his feet out from under him and slammed him crashing face down on the floor. The impact sent the fellow's hat rolling and left him floundering and half-stunned. Again, Larkin fixed his bitter glance on Roderick while laying out a final ultimatum.

"Either you walk out of here with me, or you'll be carried out on a board. The choice is yours. Make up your mind!"

Deadly portent lay behind the words, but Roderick was still sure of the odds. He held to his pose of superiority with his reply carrying its usual sardonic mockery.

"Better back away, Larkin. You forgot how to count. There's quite a few of us, but only one on your side!"

Missing no part of the showdown, Orde Fraser now made his own swift move, driving through the crowd, shouldering men out of his way. He stepped over the puncher still sprawled on the floor and took place beside the marshal.

"Make another count, Roderick," he rapped curtly. "It comes up two of us!"

A rising growl of protest had followed Fraser because of the rough way in which he had driven through the crowd. But now, as the full significance of his move and words registered, the growl of protest frittered out. A breathless pause settled over the room, soon broken by Dan Larkin, who came half around, startled and harsh.

"What is this? Nobody asked you to move in!"

"True enough," agreed Fraser evenly. "Yet, I'm here. For two reasons. One, because I like the way you're playing this hand. The other, because I've something to say and this is the time and place to say it!"

Hard-shelled and wholly unafraid of any odds though he was, Dan Larkin was also shrewdly wise in the ways and motives of men. So now he nodded, his expression impassive.

"If it's about what I think it is, go ahead — have your say."

Turk Roderick's hot stare bored at Orde Fraser. "Could be," he sneered, "that nobody is interested in listening. I'm one of such."

"Not interested, or afraid, Roderick?" retorted Fraser. He swung a quick glance around a room that was hanging intently on every word now. "Here are the facts. I'm on the store porch with Butterfield when the dragging and shooting was going on. The last two shots were not at the poor devil on the end of the rope — they were at me!"

He put a scathing, challenging glance on the Rolling C crowd. "It had to be one of you brave buckos who threw those sneak shots out of the dark. Maybe that same so brave and gallant whelp would like to step out and make another try — now! Face to face! No? . . . Well that generally figures so with such a breed. I'm new on this range and I didn't come looking for trouble. But if trouble is thrown at me, I'll meet it and take care of it in my own way. I'll be as friendly as I'm allowed to be — and as rough as I have to be. One final word — and mark it well . . . I don't carry a gun just because I like the weight of it!"

Fraser turned back to Dan Larkin. "Obliged, marshal — for letting me get that off my chest. Now I'd like to help escort friend Roderick to the lockup. And make it exactly as you told him. He can walk out or be carried out! . . ."

Before Larkin could answer, a new voice broke in. "More and more I like the sound of that proposition. And want to see it done!"

With these words, Starr Jennette left his chair and came forward to stand at the marshal's other hand. His smile was slight, the glint in his eyes cool and steady.

Again Dan Larkin's exclamation rose wrathfully. "May I be everlastingly damned! Everybody out to tell me my business. As though I couldn't handle it myself. . . ."

"Just making sure, Dan — just making sure," soothed Jennette.

Seeing no point in further argument, Larkin growled his consent. "All right, if you two are so damned bound to mix in. And Roderick — you see how it is? For the last time, I'll take that shoulder gun of yours!"

The arrogant flare still smoldered in Turk Roderick's eyes, but the truculent confidence had ebbed. Now, too, from still another weighty source came further support of the marshal. Pete Eagle spoke from across the bar.

"Better go peaceful, Turk. A lot of us see Dan Larkin as the law in this town."

Again, Roderick's hot glance raked the room. Nowhere, aside from his crew, did he see any evidence of support. Even his crew were hang-dog. The puncher Dan Larkin had laid low was now back on his feet, but considerably the worse for wear. He had hit the floor face down, and the contact had smeared his face with crimson and left him with a blank, half-dazed stare in his eyes.

Basically, behind the front of a dominating belligerence, Turk Roderick was a crafty man, a sly schemer who, so far as was possible, planned all his moves shrewdly while calculating the odds carefully before taking a stand. He measured them now and the answer came up wrong. So, even though Dan Larkin's blunt challenge and intent was gall and wormwood to him. Roderick accepted the inevitability of the moment. He gulped the rest of his whiskey, shrugged, reached under his jumper and brought out his gun. He handed it over together with final words of threat and bluster.

"This thing doesn't end here, Larkin." His turgid glance touched Orde Fraser and Starr Jennette in turn. "Which also takes care of both of you so-wise ones, as you'll damn well find out! All right, Larkin — let's go!"

Thick, sloping shoulders swinging truculently, he swaggered toward the door. Dan Larkin fell in behind him, jerking a nod to Orde Fraser.

"No place for you, now. Come along."

Together they followed Roderick into the street. As they disappeared, one of Roderick's crew blurted a curse and started after them. Starr Jennette's curt order hit the fellow like a club and stopped him in his tracks.

"No, you don't, Rube! Stay put. You're not going anywhere!"

Squat, thick-legged, charged with a surly, wicked malevolence, Rube Yard came around, the roll of his lips lifting and quivering like the snarl of a rampant animal. Starr Jennette's smile grew ever colder and thinner until there was no chance of mistaking the stern purpose behind it. Smartly recognizing all the certain signs, Pete Eagle skidded a clutch of glasses and a couple of bottles along the bar.

"Everybody up! It's on the house."

It was the right move at the right time, and brought men quickly to the bar. Two of the Rolling C crew grabbed Rube Yard, jerked him around and hauled him up beside them. Waiting out a measuring moment, Starr Jennette took a place farther along.

The Humboldt City jail consisted of three small cells back in a far corner of the courthouse basement. While the marshal marched his prisoner to one of these, Orde Fraser brought the office lamp to a full glow, then rolled a cigarette. Returning to the office, Marshal Dan Larkin walked with a step that dragged tiredly, and his face was drawn and seamed with harsh lines. Observing, Fraser made quiet comment.

"Mean night, marshal — mean all the way around."

Sighing, Larkin dropped into the chair behind the desk. "Seems there's no limit to human cussedness. Sure wears a man down. Makes him wonder if there's anything in the world worthwhile."

He lifted a gun from his coat pocket and laid it on the desk. It was the one he had taken from Turk Roderick. Orde Fraser leaned closer.

"Mind if I look it over?"

Larkin hunched a shoulder. "Go ahead."

The weapon was a short-barreled .38–40 Bisley Model Colt. Fraser flipped open the loading gate and emptied the cylinder of cartridges. After which he examined the bore of the gun carefully.

From a desk drawer, Dan Larkin had come up with a well-used pipe and a pouch of Burley fine cut. He loaded the pipe, ran a blazing match across the bowl and leaned back, puffing contentedly. Some of the hard lines in his face began to smooth out as he watched Fraser.

"Clean and unfired, of course," he observed. "Knew it would be so. Turk Roderick didn't do any shooting tonight personally. Didn't drag Shep Riley, either. He's much too sly to pull such dirty tricks personally when he can hire them done for him by somebody else. Man you're looking for would be one of his crew. Somebody like Ike Britt or Rube Yard. Two of a kind, that pair, and bad all the way through."

Reclaiming the gun and cartridges, Dan Larkin dropped them in a desk drawer. After which he fixed Orde Fraser with a narrowed glance and made further gruff comment.

"Appreciated your moving in, back there at the Ten High. But even though you expressed yourself plenty good and strong, I'm afraid you did yourself little good. Because you're a marked man, now — and you've seen what can happen to anybody Turk Roderick wants out of the way. I'm going to worry about you."

"No need," Fraser protested. "I can take care of myself. By the way, how about that fellow Jennette?"

Larkin mused on this while running a freshening match across his pipe, then spoke slowly.

"Starr Jennette is one of those you'll probably have to argue with over that Shoshone Lake range. Turk Roderick hates his guts, and has the compliment returned — in spades! They've been that way for years, even though Jennette was one of Buck Christiansen's favorite people. Choosing between them, I'd have to take Jennette. Was he to give me his word on anything, I'd be inclined to accept it. Which is more than I can say for Roderick. Incidentally, Starr Jennette is pure streaked hell with a gun. So you see, friend, you're getting a wild introduction to this stretch of country and some of the people in it."

Fraser grinned crookedly. "For a fact, I've known quieter times and places. But tell me — what would a big outfit like Rolling C have against a lone little fellow like Shep Riley?"

"Claimed he'd been careless with their beef," Larkin said. "Oldest stall in the world for getting rid of a man. Earlier today they tried to run him down but he beat them to this office. I figured to let him hole up here until they got tired of hanging around. Then, real late tonight he could slip out and away. That was my idea. Turk Roderick had a different one."

"You didn't believe he'd tampered with Rolling C beef?"

"Gave him the benefit of the doubt," Larkin explained gruffly. "Besides, he was just a skinny, scared little brush popper trying to scratch out what passed for a living on the narrow edge of nowhere. Man like him has as much right to live as some big, rich outfit. You know, friend, there's times when I wonder if Turk Roderick hasn't more on his mind than a stray beef or two. Maybe he's been looking clear past such as Shep Riley to something a lot more valuable. By the way, how did your visit with Julie Christiansen turn out?"

Fraser used a sober moment to twist up another Durham cigarette. "Sort of 'yes' and 'no,'" he said slowly. "Given a little time, things could work out all right. It's something to tackle one day at a time."

"Generally the best way to tackle any tough chore," Larkin approved. "You going back on the street tonight?"

"Only enough to get to my room."

"Smart idea." Larkin laid aside his pipe and yawned. "Get at it."

Orde Fraser met no one on his way to the hotel, nor did he see anyone there as he crossed the lobby and climbed the stairs. Pausing at the door of his room, his glance ran along the dimly lighted hallway. Here, too, all was quiet, the entire hotel having settled down for the night. Once in his room he lit the bracket lamp and let his thoughts run. Things certainly were as Dan Larkin had said. His introduction to the town and its people had been charged with explosive violence, with

57

promise of more of the same to come.

He moved to the window and looked down at a dark and now utterly quiet street, finding it a little difficult to believe that a man had been dragged to death down there and that hostile, treacherous lead had come his way out of the now peaceful dark. Still earlier, there had been the raw, brutal, physical conflict beside the stage in front of Wash Butterfield's store. Such were the shades of violence the town had so far shown him.

Reaching for more pleasant thoughts in place of these sinister ones, he made a restless turn about the room. And his thoughts turned to the girl who had been in this room not very long ago. A girl who, earlier in the evening, had shown him the bluntest kind of hostility, yet later had sought him out as a refuge from what appeared to be some sort of romantic predicament, an affair flavored with intriguing mystery. Right there she had stood, slim and appealing, with the lamplight glinting on the rich luxury of her hair, her presence a warm, disturbing thing. Such had been another of this day's happenings. . . .

Fraser shook his head, trying to free it of this tangle of conflicting facts that left a man guessing at answers and finding no good ones at all. In sudden decision he propped a chair against the door, doffed his clothes, put out the light and crawled into bed. Whatever the necessary answers, they would have to wait.

Morning's light, spilling through the window, brought Orde Fraser awake and up on one elbow. Lifting from the hotel kitchen came the fragrance of frying bacon and steaming coffee to urge him quickly from his blankets and into his clothes, all moves stirring up soreness as potent reminders of last night's harsher moments. Bending stiffly to pull on his boots caused him to grunt and softly swear at the punishment.

He drank thirstily at the big white pitcher before filling the matching bowl for a vigorous wash. Night's chill had tempered the water so it quickly cleared away the last dregs of sleep. Urged on by raw hunger, he limped downstairs. In the dining room, one of the Indian girls was cleaning up after some earlier customer who had eaten and departed. Only one other diner was present. Nell Viney sat at the side table nearest the kitchen door. She waved Fraser up, eyeing him severely.

"Sit down," she ordered curtly. "I've something to say to you!"

Orde Fraser grinned as he swung a chair around. "All right if I eat while I listen? I'm wolf hungry."

"Of course. Though I'd like to starve all you miserable male critters. What are you, anyhow? Legitimate members of the human race or the off-scourings of some ancient savagery?"

"Referring to last night's affair, of course?" Fraser murmured.

"What else?"

The Indian girl put hot coffee at Fraser's elbow. He cradled the cup in one hand and looked across at Nell Viney. "For a fact, that dragging deal was hard to take."

"Hard to take! It was inhuman, barbaric!" Nell Viney stormed. "The brutes responsible should be taken out and hung!"

"Just so," Fraser approved. "On that we agree. But why put the spurs to me, good lady? I had nothing to do with it."

"I know," was the sultry admission. "And not what I really want to talk to you about."

Now the Indian girl put hot food on the table. Fraser dug in eagerly. "Go ahead — I'm listening."

Nell Viney's next words were slow, her tone sober. "Been hearing things about you. Understand you're claiming an inheritance that is certain to cause trouble. Well, it happens there is someone else with inheritance troubles. A person I am very fond of, and I won't have you fighting with her."

Fraser's glance lifted. "Referring to Miss Julia Christiansen?"

"None other. And with that poor girl hardly knowing which way to turn, I'll not have her hounded or bullied by you or anybody else!"

Fraser lifted a protesting hand. "Good lady, I'm not out to threaten or bully Julia Christiansen in the slightest. All I ask is that her cattle be moved off my Shoshone Lake range. It's that simple."

"Sounds simple, but it's not," Nell Viney differed. "Julie won't order it done, because she can't. Which is what you must understand."

"Whoa up!" Fraser drawled. "Maybe I'm extra thickheaded this fine morning. So I have to ask — why can't she? She owns Rolling C, doesn't she?"

"She owns it, but has no voice in running it — not right now."

Orde Fraser reared back in his chair. "Lady, what kind of double-talk is that? It don't make sense."

"When you understand," stated Nell Viney vigorously, "you'll see it makes all kind of sense. And you can quit calling me — lady! As it happens I am a very proper one, but in these parts I am just Nell, and prefer it so."

The half-smile playing about Orde Fraser's lips became a chuckle. "Fair enough. Now what about this girl who owns a ranch but doesn't own it?"

"The blame," Nell Viney explained simply, "rests on a man now dead. On Buckley Christiansen, Julie's father. He was an arrogant, domineering, pig-headed old reprobate and, when he chose to be, meaner than a crippled bobcat. He built up a big, rich ranch, established a sound and prosperous bank and made himself a power in this end of the state. Proud

61

of what he had achieved, he wanted to make sure it would endure after he was gone. And he was smart enough to realize that in his climb to power and pelf, he'd left some bitter enemies along the trail.

"With no other kin, he willed it all to Julie. But he had it in his bull head that because she was daughter instead of a son, she wouldn't be able to manage Rolling C affairs until she was at least twenty-five years old. So he had that condition written into his will. Therefore, until she reaches twenty-five, which she won't for another three years, the bank is to be run by Henry Greer and the ranch by Turk Roderick."

Pausing, Nell Viney frowned down at her coffee cup, took a sip at it, then lifted her glance and went on.

"No doubt Buck Christiansen felt he could fully trust these two men, and where Henry Greer is concerned, I fully agree. But with Turk Roderick, especially after last night's ghastly affair, I say no — no, and no again! Meanwhile, Julie, poor youngster, is caught in the middle. Also, there's another angle of trouble Buck Christiansen fostered on his daughter, thinking he knew more about her personal thoughts and feelings than she knew herself. But that part is strictly Julie's own affair and none of mine. It is something she'll have to find the answer to in her own way. So, now that you know, I expect you to be as generous and patient toward her as you can."

Having had her say, Nell Viney scooped up her empty dishes and headed kitchenward, yet pausing for a backward look and final word.

"If you figure me a nosy old gossip, you could be right. But remember this. Everything I just told you is the gospel truth!"

Throughout the balance of his meal, Orde Fraser had plenty to think about. Recalling the several moods and moves he had encountered in Julia Christiansen, he now found them easier to understand. Here was a young woman, scarcely out of girlhood, who was the owner of a bank and a big, powerful cattle ranch, and who, as such, was basically responsible for the acts and public status of both, yet had no direct hand in the management of either. Small wonder that at one time or another he had found her cold, hostile, harried, confused, softly shy — and even at times, more than anything else, little-kid scared. . . .

Leaning back in his chair he built a Durham cigarette, his thoughts turning wry. From every angle it was increasingly apparent that he had inherited a great deal more than just a stretch of cattle range. He beckoned the Indian girl to his side, and asked a question.

"The bank opens at ten in the morning?"

Told that it did, he moved out to the porch and selected a chair. The street before him lay empty, the town itself almost too quiet. It was, he mused, like it was hiding a shamed face after last night's show of raw savagery.

Out yonder the Humboldt Rim reared its massiveness, no less grim and impressive than it had appeared under last night's starlight. Now, in the pour of the morning sun, it seemed to reflect a sort of sullen glow, with its many faces standing out dark and hard-angled. The great scarp dominated all the world round about. Also, Fraser thought, it certainly reduced man and all his petty doings to puny insignificance.

Distant on the sage flats, a tawny banner of dust marked the progress of a double-hitch freight outfit starting its long haul out to Iron Mountain. Down street a gaunt, old, red-tick hound dog came into view and made his slow, ambling, doggy way along, pausing leisurely to sniff here and there. Coming even with the hotel, he spied Fraser and climbed the porch steps and moved to Fraser's side, wagging a friendly tail. In response to a pat on the head, the dog smeared Fraser's hand with a lolling tongue then settled wearily down, sighing its great content.

Grinning, Fraser murmured, "That's it, old feller. You and me, we'll take it easy while we wait this thing out. . . ."

CHAPTER IV

Henry Greer was a neat, precise man. His features were thin, his hair white. Showing typical banker caution when facing a stranger, his attitude was guarded as he studied the draft Orde Fraser presented. That same reserve was in his eyes when his glance lifted to the man on the other side of the wicket.

"You wish to deposit this and so open an account?"

Orde Fraser nodded. "That's it."

Again Henry Greer studied the draft, in particular the signature it carried. "L. J. Blackwell," he murmured. "That would have to be Lester Jason Blackwell, more familiarly known in banking circles as Long Les Blackwell?"

"So I've heard." Fraser's tone carried a small edge of impatience. "Do you question the soundness of the draft?"

"Oh, no — not at all — not at all," Henry Greer assured him hastily. "You — er — work for Mr. Blackwell?"

"No, just for myself. Now, how's for setting up the account, so I can draw on it and be on my way? I've a lot of things to do."

Fifteen minutes later Orde Fraser was back on the street, heading for the courthouse. Morning's sunlight, slanting through the cotton-woods, had already begun to lay down a touch of warmth. Over on the towering rim crest, the freight outfit was just topping out at the head of the grade and, against the rim's immensity, both wagons and mules were reduced to Lilliputian proportions.

Appearing in the doorway of his office, Marshal Dan Larkin offered gruff greeting. "Thought by this time you'd be long gone out to that Shoshone Lake range of yours."

"Had to wait for the bank to open," Fraser explained. "Needed money to buy a horse. Got any suggestions?"

Larkin yawned and stretched, grumbling. "Don't get over a bad night as easy as I used to. Must be getting old. A horse, you say? Well, Benny Rust should have something in his stable corral to interest you. But watch yourself. All things considered, Benny's not a bad sort. But he's a born trader, and a shrewd one."

Fraser smiled faintly. "Met up with such before. Generally manage to hold my own. All right if I collect my gear?"

Larkin stepped aside. "It's right where you left it."

Fraser shouldered his saddle, tucked his rifle under his arm. "How's the prisoner doing?"

Larkin shrugged. "Quiet, so far."

"How long do you figure to hold him?"

"Until he gets it through his arrogant skull that I run this town. Incidentally, when he is

66

loose again, I suggest you keep an eye on your back trail."

Heading away, Orde Fraser said, "Already had that figured."

Benny Rust was short and round. He had a moon face and guileless blue eyes. His too-large bib overalls were sagging and soiled and much the worse for wear and tear. A well-chewed toothpick revolved in one corner of his mouth and his voice was high and piping.

"Horses for sale? Sure — whole corral full. What you looking for, a cattle-working bronc or just a good trail horse? You name it — I got it."

Some two dozen animals were in the corral. Only two held Orde Fraser's glance for more than a moment. One was a solid, short-coupled, line-backed dun with the look of both speed and endurance about it. The other was a gray, also well put together.

Missing no indication of interest on Fraser's part, Benny Rust made quick suggestion. "Yonder gray is as good an all-around bronc as any man could want."

"How much?" Fraser asked.

"Seventy-five. And worth every cent of it."

Fraser climbed the fence. "I'll have a closer look."

He cornered the gray, quieted it, ran a hand over it here and there. He did the same with the dun, then came back to the fence.

"Give you sixty for the dun."

Benny Rust's blue-eyed glance flickered. "The gray's the one I was talking about."

"I know," Orde Fraser drawled. "But you forgot to mention a sweenied off-shoulder. Give you sixty for the dun."

"That's pure robbery!" Benny shrilled.

Fraser shrugged. "Sixty is my offer."

Benny kept trying. "Sixty-five?"

"Sixty."

Benny caved. "You win." He eyed Fraser with a resentful respect. "Bought yourself a horse. Best one in the corral. Been around some, haven't you?"

Fraser grinned. "Some."

He counted out the sixty. One golden double eagle, four golden eagles. "And a bill of sale, of course."

"You sure have been around," Benny declared, leaving to scribble one.

Leading the dun from the corral, Fraser saddled it. "Shoshone Lake." He questioned, "where and how far?"

Benny Rust jerked an indicating thumb. "Maybe six, seven miles."

"What kind of country?"

Benny considered, lips pursed. "Good range. Plenty of grass . . . Plenty of water. Few stretches of badlands lava. Why you asking?"

"Because I own it."

So saying, Orde Fraser hung his rifle under his near stirrup fender, swung astride and started to rein away, then hauled the dun to a halt, his glance reaching up street at a slim figure that had just left the hotel and was crossing to the bank. There was no mistaking that dark-honey head, or the proud carriage of it, shining in the sun. Again the present contrast of the street with what it had been last night struck through and a shadowed gravity pulled at Fraser's cheeks.

Benny Rust caught the same thought. "Hard to figure," he piped soberly. "Everything so mild and pretty now. But last night — man!" He glanced toward the mouth of the stable runway. "Shep Riley's still in there. Never amounted to much, Shep didn't. Maybe a time or two he might have cut a steak off'n a stray beef, but he never did anything to deserve what was done to him. Gives a man to wonder why they drug him. Yessir, gives a man to wonder. . . ." Benny wagged an uneasy head.

Fraser watched Julie Christiansen until she disappeared into the bank, then reined on out of town. Right away he found he'd not wasted his sixty dollars. This horse under him was strong, willing and easy gaited. Recalling how he had traveled yesterday, Fraser found it fine to be in the saddle again. A stage, he mused, might carry a man, yet was an inert, mechanical thing, fashioned of wood and iron and so totally unresponsive and devoid of life and feeling. But a horse — ah, that was something different! A horse was warm flesh and blood, owning a vital current of life and a spirit to reach up and communicate with its rider. A good horse was a partner, a companion. The whole world looked better from the back of a horse. From here a man was more conscious of freedom and space. All these stray fancies to meditate on and revel in before recalling Dan Larkin's parting advice about keeping an alert eye on his back trail.

Advice he now took, twisting in his saddle for a survey of the land behind him. Distance had already reduced Humboldt City to a patch of huddled cottonwood greenery. Towering above it, turning smoky with haze, the Humboldt Rim marched its great curve, walling off all the world beyond. This was high desert country; wild, lonely and remote, blanketed with gray-green sage that lifted its pungent breath into the steadily warming air.

In time, as the miles fell behind, the dun began breasting a gradual, up-running slope toward a distant, low crest. And when, presently, he topped this crest, Orde Fraser knew he was looking out across the Shoshone Lake range, as the land immediately ahead became a down slope into a wide basin of grass country. It was a land of many trails, cut by the cattle he now began to pass. Along with other values it was evident that this was good calving ground, for numbers of the little white-faces scampered about, followed by anxious, lowing mothers. Off to one side a ponderous herd bull dozed in solitary dignity.

As he rode, Fraser read brands, with the Rolling C in strong evidence on all sides. A couple of critters carried the S–J Connected, suggesting the name of Starr Jennette. Fraser counted a single Rafter D and two others were Bar HW. Regardless of brands, all the stock were in prime condition, hides sleek and shining.

Presently the dun fell into a trail more deeply cut than the others, one which led directly into the far reaches of the basin. Here, in time, a low spine of lava lifted to bar the way. Paralleling this barrier, the trail finally circled the far end of it, and it was now quickly apparent why this trail had seen such heavy use. Out there ahead spread several acres of rippling lake water.

Marsh grass and tules fringed the lake's edge and against these green shades the red and white hides of several beef critters stood out in strong contrast. The nearest of these, a chunky yearling, spooked by Fraser's approach, surged wildly away, startling a pair of mallard ducks into flight from a nearby nook, and the drake's head was a climbing emerald jewel against the sunlit sky.

Following the shore line, the trail led into a stretch of meadow that ran back to another spine of lava. Crouched against this, as though for shelter or support, was a small, weather-beaten cabin whose rusty stovepipe gave off a thin drift of wood smoke. Closing in, Orde Fraser wondered about that smoke and the cause for it.

It was a wonder short-lived. A man's gaunt figure filled the cabin doorway. The rifle he carried came swiftly up and the report was a hard, rocketing pound across a startled world. Slightly ahead of Fraser and to one side of the trail, a clump of sod was ripped up. The echoes of the shot, rolling flatly into empty distance, were followed by a harsh-voiced order.

"You can stop right there!"

Orde Fraser did not argue the point. Set sharply back, the dun jigged nervously while Fraser, high in his saddle, kept careful watch of the man who now stepped fully into the clear; rifle poised and ready for a second shot. Came further harsh words.

"Turn around and get the hell out! Go on back to Rolling C and tell your boss he's all through rawhiding Poe Darby!"

The rifle settled dead in line with Fraser's high-reared figure. "You heard me! Go on back and tell Turk Roderick what I said!"

Orde Fraser kept his reply quiet and steady. "Friend, you got me all wrong. I don't ride for Rolling C."

The owner of the rifle came forward, ink-black eyes boring at Fraser. This was a lank and thin and hawk-faced old man; burned black and leathery by long seasons of sun and wind and weather. He made careful measure of Fraser before speaking again, still harshly.

"I'm getting this straight before I take my gun off you. If you ain't ridin' for Rolling C,

72

who the hell are you riding for?"

"For myself — strictly!" Fraser told him. "I'm new here, and taking my first look at the country. Name's Fraser — Orde Fraser."

Alert belligerence lessened, rifle muzzle lowering as the owner of it spoke. "Now that I look closer, I see you're a stranger. But I know that horse you're up on. Saw it last in Benny Rust's corral."

"Right," Fraser affirmed. "I bought the dun this morning from Benny." He tipped a shoulder toward the cabin. "Yours?"

"No. Shep Riley's. I come in early this morning wanting to see Shep about something. I figgered he'd be back before long, so I boiled up a pot of coffee while waitin' for him to show."

"Long wait, Old Timer," Fraser said soberly. "Too long. Shep Riley isn't going to show here. Not now — not ever! . . ."

About to move away, the old fellow whirled back. "What's that you're sayin'? That Shep ain't comin' back! What do you mean?"

"Just that," Fraser told him. "Shep Riley is dead. They killed him in town last night. A Rolling C hand named Ike Britt dragged him to death."

For a long moment the old man was very still. Then a strange, wild look came over him. His black eyes glittered, became intent and fierce. "You wouldn't just be talkin'?"

"I wish it was that way, but it isn't," Fraser

said. "I was there and I saw it happen. Ike Britt dragged Shep Riley to death right down the middle of the street in Humboldt City."

The old fellow pulled himself up very straight while staring off into the distance, as though envisioning something hostile and threatening, and bracing himself against it. His words fell low and bitter.

"They'll never quit until they get it all! They burned out Andy Quider and they burned out me. They burned out Shep Riley, and now they've killed him. They got Hollis Ward so stampeded he's ready to sell out for a dime on the dollar. It's that fellow Roderick — that rotten, damned Turk Roderick! He's out to grab it all!"

Again the old man stared off into the distance with that strange, wild intentness. Then he shook himself and, as his glance came back to Fraser, his words were apologetic.

"Forgettin' my manners," he said simply. "I'm Poe Darby. Been in these parts a long time — mebbe too long. But I'll hang on longer, now. Because Shep Riley was my friend — and they killed him. Somebody pays me for that! I know this country — every damn inch of it. I can make a siwash camp in the worst part of it and still get along if I have to. I can lay in wait until I get somebody of that Rolling C crowd over the sights of this!" He patted his rifle. "When I do, Rolling C comes up short on its crew tally. They can call it drygulchin' —

they can call it any damn thing they want, but it's the only way left for a feller like me."

Again he shook himself, as though to get free of bitter, burning thoughts. To Fraser he said, "Light down and come in. Else the coffee will be boiled plumb away."

Fraser ground-reined the dun horse and followed inside. The cabin was small and poor, but neat enough. Noting Fraser's interest, Poe Darby shrugged, explaining.

"Was a line camp in the old days. Yance Milliken built it. Good spot for a line camp, being close to water and all. Was empty for a long time before Shep Riley moved in. It was after Rolling C burned Shep out of his old place that he came here. Now they've killed him, probably figgerin' on puttin' somebody of their own here. They try that, they'll have to get past me! You say it was Ike Britt who did the draggin'?"

"That's how Dan Larkin and Wash Butterfield named him."

Poe Darby bobbed a gaunt head. "Then it must be so. Dan and Wash are both good men." He poured coffee; handed Orde Fraser a cup. It was strong and black. Fraser looked past the rim of his cup.

"You knew Yance Milliken?"

Again the gaunt head bobbed. "Knew him well. Knew Buckley Christiansen just as well. Them two fellers had a rough feud over this piece of range, back and forth. Little fellers like me got caught in between. When feudin' just between the two of them, Yance Milliken and Buck Christiansen were meaner than sore-eared bears. But where us little fellers were concerned, they weren't bad at all. Both Yance and Buck treated me fair and decent, and I liked 'em. When Yance up and died, old Buck Christiansen had it all to himself, but he still left us little fellers alone. But when Buck died and Turk Roderick took over, all hell busted loose. They tell me that Buck Christiansen's daughter owns everything now. But it is Turk Roderick who handles all Rolling C affairs . . . and he's one greedy, no-good, crooked whelp!"

Orde Fraser sorted out his next words carefully. "Suppose I were to tell you that this Shoshone Lake range now belongs to me — what would you think?"

So startled he spilled hot coffee on his hand, Poe Darby swore his amazement. "Be damned! Wouldn't know what to think!"

"Yet it's a fact," Fraser stated, going on to tell of his relationship with Yance Milliken and the inheritance that had come to him because of it. "I can see I've inherited trouble as well as range," he ended. "So I could use considerable help from someone who knows the country and the people in it. If you and this Andy Quider you speak of should happen to be interested enough to ride with me, that would surely be my good fortune. You'll draw top wages and if we make it stick, you'll have all you had before, plus a lot more."

Poe Darby turned the proposition over in his mind for a little time before putting a stern, penetrating glance on Orde Fraser, as though he would see completely through him while measuring his every thought and purpose. What he saw seemed to satisfy him, for he nodded gruffly.

"It's a deal. Never was one to bet blind, and when I go plumb out to the end of a limb for a man, I want to be sure he'll be right there with me. You got the look of being that kind of a man. We won't worry none about money. What I want, more than anything else, is a fair chance to even up with that damn Turk Roderick and his crowd. You served notice on them yet?"

"Last night in town," Fraser nodded. "And got shot at twice from the dark."

"From the dark, eh?" Poe Darby snorted. "Well that's the way they operate, now that Turk Roderick is callin' the turns. Put a match to a man's cabin when he ain't around. Try to gun him from the dark, or drag him to death when they got all the odds." He turned back to the stove. "Right now I'm hungry enough to put a bait of grub together. The water bucket needs fillin' and there's a spring out back past the corral."

Smiling to himself, Orde Fraser took the bucket and went out. That abrupt, crusty old fellow in there was just the sort he was looking

77

for. Smart and fierce, tough and enduring as seasoned rawhide.

The lean-to stable at the rear of the cabin was big enough for two horses and the corral beyond would hold a dozen if needful. At the moment it held only Poe Darby's mount; a rangy, blue roan. Off to one side in a shadowed pocket of the lava ridge a spring bubbled up, clear and sweet and cold, it's constant overflow finding its way to the lake.

In the cabin Poe Darby had freshened his fire, sliced bacon, and was mixing up a pan of dough-god biscuits. With these in the oven he rinsed the coffee pot and spooned in a fresh supply while speaking across his shoulder.

"No better water in the world than from that spring. Makes the best coffee I know of. Yance Milliken's father sure knew his business when he wangled that Indian grant."

In time the coffee steamed, bacon sputtered to crispness in the pan and biscuits came out of the oven, hot and brown and crusty. Over this good fare Poe Darby asked questions and Orde Fraser gave him all the answers. And added a warning.

"The odds may be a little heavy at first, but help is on the way from outside, together with a fair-sized herd of white-faces to start us going. Finally, considering an angle you saw and mentioned, let's take another look at it. You say Rolling C burned out you and Quider and Shep Riley. Then, when Riley settled here, making talk about him being a rustler, they killed him. But they didn't burn this cabin, which suggests they could have ideas about using it themselves. So — watch it!" Fraser warned. "You sure Quider will be interested?"

"Plumb!" Poe Darby emphasized. "Andy's not much bigger than a pint of Pete Eagle's whiskey. But he's a feisty little cuss who'll do a man's work at anything you put him to — 'specially when the blue chips are down. Likewise and besides, he's just as anxious as I am to gouge a chunk out of Turk Roderick's hide. I'll have him here tomorrow morning."

Standing in the doorway, Orde Fraser spun up a Durham cigarette. "And I'll be here in the morning with a supply of grub and other gear."

As Fraser headed for his horse, Poe Darby came out and called after him. "What kind of fodder does that rifle of yours take?"

Fraser slapped the holstered gun at his hip. "Same as this. Forty-fours."

"Just right!" Poe approved. "Same as mine and Andy's. But no good without plenty of fodder. Better have Wash Butterfield add a few boxes of forty-fours to the rest of the gear."

"An idea," Fraser agreed. "While here's a thought for you. This place is home to us now. Don't let them burn it on us!"

"Ha!" Poe growled. "Let 'em try. Will they learn somethin'!"

Fraser rode out along the same trail he'd come in on. A small, warm wind, pushing past the fringe of tules, had the lake waters dancing. The pair of mallards, resting well out from shore, bobbed up and down. A flock of blackbirds, only lately winged in, balanced on swaying tule tips and set up a bright and tinkling chorus. Cattle coming in to water passed Fraser, some fairly close, others swinging wide of him.

Orde Fraser's thoughts were on the place he'd just left. Taken all together, it represented a layout with opportunities much greater than just a setting for a frugal little line camp. Here, given time and opportunity, a man could fashion an entire ranch headquarters. Here a man could plant his roots deep and permanent. For the place had everything. . . .

As he rode, the mind picture grew and brightened steadily. . . .

CHAPTER V

Though her head had been high while crossing the street, the moment Julie Christiansen entered the Humboldt City Bank, her step faltered and she became a smaller figure, subdued and forlorn. Pushing aside some paper work, Henry Greer came to his feet, exclaiming his pleasure.

"Julie! Girl — girl, you've been away from us too long!"

"And wishing now I hadn't come back," was the muffled, half-tearful reply. "I — I just learned what really happened last night. I knew there was a ruckus of some sort as I heard shouting and several gunshots, but I was so very tired I went to sleep in spite of it all. At late breakfast this morning, Nell Viney told me what really happened — what had happened to Shep Riley. And it was Rolling C riders who did that ghastly thing. You hear, Henry? Men of my own ranch did it. The cruelest, most brutally savage thing I ever heard of. And I'm sickened! I'll never be able to look a decent person in the eye again as long as I live — not ever!"

The last words were a small, thin wail. She dropped into a chair and huddled there, her expression haunted, her tear-wet eyes dark and stormy with feeling.

Too honest to attempt to minimize a thing that could not be minimized, Henry Greer's answer was quietly direct. "Most certainly a foul, brutal happening, which I cannot understand Turk Roderick allowing. I understand your feelings, but being in no way responsible, you mustn't punish yourself too severely."

Henry Greer had known Julie Christiansen since she was a pigtailed stripling; one who, while very young, had lost her mother. He himself, a kindly bachelor and long-time friend and confidant of Buckley Christiansen, while watching Julie grow up and move into young womanhood, had come to know a fatherly concern for her and all her affairs. Looking at her now, so crushed and tearful, he recalled words Buck Christiansen had spoken when on his deathbed.

"Henry," the old cattleman had said, "look after our girl. It comes to me now that I might have done better by her than I have. I leave her with plenty of the material things of life, but also, now that I'm about to go, I've left her with certain enmities to be faced alone. So I've called on Turk Roderick, my long-time foreman, to run the rougher ranch affairs and on you to handle the bank and all financial affairs until Julie is mature enough to take over and manage for herself. I've meant nothing but the best for her, yet I'm wondering if I've done the right things in the right way. Yeah, I'm wondering!"

And so Buckley Christiansen had died — still wondering.

Bowed in her chair, Julie shook a disconsolate head that denied Henry Greer's well-meant, comforting words. "But I am responsible. I am responsible for all that Rolling C does. I am responsible for what was done to poor Shep Riley, and over that I must punish myself. If it would do any good I'd weep a bucket of tears for Shep Riley, but that wouldn't help, either. I'd like to hit out at those who killed him — I'd like to strike them somehow! . . ."

She broke off with a gust of feeling that seemed to come out of nowhere with such strange suddenness as to leave her half-breathless — a gust of feeling and purpose that fired her next words with a small fierceness.

"Henry, I'm getting rid of Turk Roderick, this very day. For some time I've not cared for his attitude of possessiveness that would at times come near to suggesting that it was he, not I, who owned the Rolling C ranch. It was one of the main reasons I went away for a time. So that I could be alone and try to think things out. I was prepared to give him another chance, but after last night I'll not have him around another hour!

"Oh, I know how Dad's will reads," she went on. "He was trying to make things easier for me, but it hasn't worked out that way at all. Nor could it — ever! And I know he wouldn't want to hold me to the exact provisions of the will after what has happened. So on this, I am determined. Turk Roderick is through at Rolling C — through for all time!"

To this Henry Greer gave sober agreement. "Which is as it should be. But it won't be easy, Julie. The man will resist in every way possible. He has an overweening arrogance that makes him very sure of himself. While you've been away I had, on several occasions, reason to remind him that the affairs of this bank were strictly none of his." The banker cleared his throat before adding, "Getting rid of Turk Roderick is only one of our problems; there could be further ones from other sources. Consider this."

He laid a strip of paper in front of Julie. She studied it, then raised her glance. "I see a bank draft for two thousand dollars, drawn on the Pioneer Standard Bank by L. J. Blackwell, in favor of one Orde Fraser. What's wrong with that?"

"The signature. L. J. Blackwell. It interests me."

Again Julie studied the draft. Again she glanced up, puzzled. "Is that so very much out of the ordinary?"

"Let's at least say that it is cause for thought," Henry Greer said. "L. J. Blackwell. Lester Jason Blackwell. Also known in banking circles as Long Les Blackwell, and rated as a man who would never have enough of anything — in particular money and power. He is also

84

known as a persistent hater who never forgets or forgives a business defeat. Long Les Blackwell who, next to Yance Milliken, was probably the most bitter and unrelenting enemy your father ever had. It was an enmity that started long ago, back when you were a very little girl. It happened in this manner. When Charley Garth — the original founder of this bank — died, the business was like a maverick beef running free on the range: a property of the first legitimate and fair buyer who came along. Long Les Blackwell was after it, hoping to buy it up cheap. Your father, Buckley Christiansen, made a fairer offer and got the prize. That built up the big hate on Long Les's part. A number of times since then he has done his best to embarrass us in a financial way, but so far without too much success. But with Long Les Blackwell there is always another time and another day. Which could be now. Take a look at the other name on the draft. It reads 'Orde Fraser,' an individual lately arrived and laying claim to the old Milliken Indian grant range through some channel of inheritance."

Julie Christiansen stirred in her chair. "That is so. He has already spoken to me about it."

"All of which is, to me, very interesting," Henry Greer said dryly. "When I add these facts up and see how they are pointing, I can't help but be interested. Because past experience with Long Les Blackwell, for me at least, points a finger at a very devious individual!"

Julie pushed a weary hand across her eyes. "Problems — problems — problems!" She drew a deep breath, came up a little straighter in her chair. "The bank and its affairs in general?"

"Sound and secure," Henry Greer assured. "You've no slightest cause for concern there."

He would have said more, but a step sounded at the door and it was Marshal Dan Larkin who entered, rumbling his greeting.

"Morning, Henry — Miss Julie!" He faced Julie. "You know about last night?"

His glance was stern, but kindly. Julie met it steadily. "I know, marshal — I know — too well! Nell Viney told me. And I'm sick at heart."

"Not your fault," comforted Larkin. "But just now I got Turk Roderick under lock and key. He did neither the actual dragging nor the shooting, but he could have stopped both had he wanted to, so I'm holding him responsible. Still and all, I can't keep him locked up forever for something he did not actually do personally. And there's no telling what kind of hell he could cook up next. Julie, that fellow is mean stuff and, frankly, is doing neither you nor your Rolling C ranch any good at all. So what's ahead?"

"This!" Julie came to her feet, her tone firming. "No matter how Dad's will reads, the fact remains that the ranch belongs to me, and me alone. So, starting now, I intend to run it as I see fit. My first act of real authority is this! I am firing Turk Roderick. Where Rolling C affairs are concerned, he is definitely all through. Something else, marshal. I am paying any and all costs of Shep Riley's funeral. And if you can locate any kin of his, I am doing something for them, also."

"Good girl!" applauded Larkin. He smiled slightly. "I go now to release Turk Roderick from durance vile."

"When you do," Julie directed, "tell him that I will see him immediately in Nell Viney's hotel parlor."

She followed Larkin into the street. A quiet street now — and pleasant under the day's warming touch. And part of a familiar world which, because of her new determination of purpose, had suddenly become a very good world to be in. Consciousness of this struck so strongly it left her exultant, slightly breathless and tiptoe eager.

Out there was the rim's long, solid face, cloaked in autumn's early haze. Round about, the leaves of the cottonwoods glimmered in the sunlight, and sparrows twittered their contentment in the greenery. Over yonder, the usual scatter of blackbirds fluttered about the overflow from Benny Rust's watering trough.

All this a part of her world — the best of all worlds — welcoming her home. . . .

Strange indeed how the reaction gripped her,

this feeling of being back where she belonged, and exulting over it. What had happened to her? Where now all the frets and worries that had haunted her? She paused in a patch of shade to ponder these questions. . . .

From what had she gained this great and wonderful surge of new confidence and decision? Had it been the shock of last night's savage, brutal affair — or was it something more? Had the change taken root when she stood in the room of a stranger last night; the room of a lean, quiet-voiced man who, in some mysterious way, had understood her fears and uncertainties and advised her on them?

Recalling the incident, her cheeks burned. What on earth had possessed her to seek refuge in that room? Instinct — intuition? Whatever it was, it had happened. And he had shown her nothing but kindness and courtesy, after she, earlier, had shown him nothing but outright enmity.

In any event, all that was of last night. And now she, Julie Christiansen, mistress of the Rolling C ranch, was also mistress of herself, prepared to face any and all responsibilities, whatever they might be, whatever the decision necessary. Cast off were all the shackles of fear and uncertainty. Now she feared nothing. Now she was free! . . .

As she moved on into the hotel, her step was buoyant and eager.

In the basement of the courthouse, Turk

Roderick emerged from his cell as surly and truculent as when he had entered it. Because of the hot malevolence scourging him he had done little sleeping. His pale eyes were bloodshot and whisker stubble roughened his heavy jaws emphasizing, rather than concealing, the staining bruises put there by Orde Fraser's fists.

However, as Wash Butterfield had remarked, this was a proud man; and though the ignominy of the hours behind bars had heightened the tempest of feeling punishing him, they had in no way humbled him. Instead the inner fires burned more hotly than ever, strengthening many inner resolves. The breakfast Dan Larkin had brought him earlier was untouched, which fact Larkin remarked on pungently.

"Man who refuses good food is a fool!"

Roderick's answer was flung like a blow. "I want no favors from you — ever! . . ."

"Which you'll get none of — not ever!" was Larkin's curt retort. "Now your boss, Julie Christiansen, is waiting for you in the hotel parlor. Get over there. She has several things to say to you."

In the marshal's office, Roderick made a hard turn. "How about my gun?"

Lifting the weapon from a drawer, Larkin skidded it across the desk. "Lucky for you it hadn't been fired last night, else it would have furnished the evidence to hang you. Your horse is at Benny Rust's livery stable, under the same

89

roof where Shep Riley lies dead. Something for you to think about when you call for the bronc. Now go see Julie Christiansen. Past that — get out of town!"

The bottled-up tumult in Turk Roderick congested his eyes and bulged the cords of his throat, but he could not sustain the cold contempt in Dan Larkin's glance. He drove out into the street and tramped along with heavy, lunging strides, pausing at the hotel steps as though making a survey of the world round about. In reality he was using the time to get a better grip on himself, knowing it would not do to face Julie Christiansen with the same ugly mood he'd shown Dan Larkin. When the inner furies quieted somewhat, he went on in — his step lighter, the swing of his shoulders carrying the old truculent, confident arrogance.

In the hotel parlor Julie Christiansen faced him with a look and manner that stirred up a thread of unease. When he spoke, his words were mild and conciliatory.

"Larkin said you wanted to see me?"

While waiting for this man to show, Julie had thought of what she intended to say, wondering if she could do it with the necessary weight of authority. It proved less difficult than she had feared, and she laid it on the line with a curt directness.

"Yes, I do. It is to tell you that you are all through as the foreman of my ranch. And before returning to ranch headquarters for your personal gear, stop in at the bank. Henry Greer will pay you off!"

Whatever Turk Roderick had expected, it was nothing as blunt and devastating as this. It set him back on his heels and brought him up staring. And though the inner fires began blazing high again, he managed a fairly mild reply.

"I don't understand. You realize what you are saying?"

"I certainly do! And mean every word of it!"

"But why — why?"

"You know why — you know exactly why!" Julie was holding nothing back. "That wicked affair last night — the cruel, cowardly murder of Shep Riley. You allowed that to happen — perhaps even ordered it done. So you will never ride again for any ranch of mine!"

Turk Roderick's first thought had been to play this thing mildly, to stall and keep the lid on until time had softened the shock, and this stormy-eyed young woman in front of him would be more amenable to what he considered to be sound reasoning. Studying her carefully now, he realized that the soft approach he had planned wouldn't do at all. The flush of outraged anger in her cheeks was too strong, and the outright aversion in her glance too unrelenting. Only a stern hitting back would do any good, he decided. And so he used it, harshly.

"Girl, you're not using your head — not

thinking straight. Shep Riley was no good, and he has been eating Rolling C beef. Your father believed in the rope for any and all cattle thieves, and so would have approved what we did. He might have merely hung Shep Riley to a limb of the nearest tree, but he sure as hell would have hung him. We just did it a handier way!"

Indignant denial of all this shaped itself on Julie's lips, but before she could speak, Roderick went on heavily.

"What we did was in the best interest of Rolling C. On this range our outfit has always been the big, fat target for all the little, sniveling coyote layouts to shoot at and feed on if allowed to get away with it. They didn't get away with it while Buck Christiansen was alive, and they don't get away with it now. Start seeing and recognizing the facts from that sensible angle, and when you've calmed down we'll talk it over again."

So saying, he turned and lurched out; thick, heavy, down-sloped shoulders swinging.

For a little time sheer frustration held Julie Christiansen quiet and still, while a shadow of the old fears and sense of helplessness hovered. Then she shook herself; her head came up and the new-born pride and purpose returned to wipe out all uncertainty. After all, the reaction of Turk Roderick was merely as Henry Greer had warned. It would not be easy to get rid of Roderick — the man was too resourceful and savagely sure of himself. But now she too was sure of herself, very sure. Whatever the means necessary to handle Roderick, those were the means she would use! . . .

She climbed to her room after her luggage. It was important that she get out to ranch head-quarters as soon as possible, to be close to all of the ranch affairs and find out first-hand what was going on. And above all, then assert her authority to any and all concerned.

Half an hour later she found Benny Rust fixing a hoof-shattered board in his corral fence. Benny came up off his knees and touched a finger to his hat.

"Miss Julie! My — oh, my — it sure is fine to have you back home and purtyin' up this old stretch of country again. You bet — sure is!"

She smiled at him. "And mighty good to be back, Benny. Now I've a lot of luggage to haul out to the ranch, so I'll need a buckboard and team. Will you bring one up to the hotel?"

"Right away," Benny said, laying his hammer aside and heading for the stable. From the mouth of the stable runway he watched Julie move back up street, head high, slim shoulders straight.

"Now that there sure is a different girl than the one who went travelin'," he observed to the world at large. "Somethin' about her now that wasn't ever there before. Mebbe it's that new spark in her eye. And she musta give Turk Roderick a high-class rawhidin' from the way he acted when he come after his horse. Me, I hope she spurs him some more!"

Julie's luggage was piled on the hotel porch when Benny arrived with the buckboard and team. Benny loaded on several gripsacks and a small, leather-bound trunk. He gave Julie a hand up to the buckboard seat and she rewarded him with another smile as she took the reins.

"I'll have one of the crew bring this rig back, Benny."

Benny touched his hat again. "Any time, Miss Julie."

The team of sorrels were fresh and eager. Once clear of town Julie let them get rid of the first edge of spirit, then held them down to an even, steady gait and sat back to enjoy the drive out to home headquarters.

Home! How much the word had suddenly come to mean, and how eager she was to see it again! A few short months ago it had been something to flee from. Now she was wishing behind her the miles of return!

Cutting through the sage, pitching up and down when crossing an occasional dry-wash, the road looped along below the towering run of the rim. Again and again Julie looked up at the face of the great scarp as though giving welcome to an old friend. Born in the shadow of this massive barrier, its brooding presence had been a part of her life down through all the years.

One stretch of the road, where it swung quite close to the base of the rim, was known as Echo Reach. As a little girl, when riding with her father to or from town, it was her habit to call out in high childish treble and listen in fascinated delight as the echo came bounding back, true and clear. She wondered how it would be to call out the echo today. It was a fancy to smile over, but nothing more.

For out there ahead, in the very heart of Echo Reach, a rider waited: a lean, dark-faced rider who held his place until she had to rein in the sorrels. He touched his hat.

"Hello, Julie! Sorry to waylay you like this, but it seemed the only chance I'd have to talk with you. It's been a long time, Julie. Too long."

She faced him gravely. Here was another part of the running-away picture that now had to be met. She kept her reply even and quiet.

"Hello, Starr. I hardly expected to find you here."

Starr Jennette shrugged. "Figured you'd be heading home some time today. Julie, I'm the same person I've always been. You don't ever have to be afraid of me or hide from me. You should know that. So why did you avoid me in the hotel last night? You were in that stranger's room, weren't you?"

Julie felt the flush that stormed up her cheeks, yet she held his dark glance steadily. "Yes, Starr — I was. And you'll never understand, anymore than I do myself, the impulse that carried me in there. If we say I was simply stampeded — still on the run — it will be as close to the truth as anything else. In any event, stranger or not, the man in that room was most kind and considerate, so you must hold nothing against him. Now there is an understanding to be arrived at between you and me. Come closer, as there are things you must know."

He touched his horse with the spur and moved up beside the buckboard. With deft fingers he fashioned a Durham cigarette and touched a flaming sulphur match to it. Through the first curl of smoke, he made gentle suggestion.

"Maybe you found some answers while you were away?"

"Some, at least," Julie nodded. "And more on returning. Since last night and this morning, Starr — silly as it may sound — I believe I've finally grown up and come to really know my own mind. I know what I want to do — what I'm going to do. Starting now, for better or worse, I will manage my own mind and my own personal affairs." Held in sober thought, she paused for a moment before going on.

"Poor Dad! He really meant well. In his extreme desire to make sure of my future welfare, he thought to arrange everything, even to matters between you and me. All of which left me with the feeling of being virtually a prisoner of sorts, caught in a web of misunderstanding and overdone concern. And somehow, some way, I had to break out. Which is why I ran, reaching for freedom and the right to be myself in all things and all ways."

"And now you believe you've found all these things?" Jennette's steady regard did not waver. Nor did Julie's as she answered.

"At least part of them, yes. The rest will follow."

Jennette looked away, taking another deep pull at his cigarette before crushing out the butt on the horn of his saddle. After which he spoke slowly, as though fearful of what he was about to hear.

"Between you and me, Julie — what's it to be?"

She told him gently, but definitely. "It won't do, Starr. It never would and never could. I've thought about it a very great deal and realize that temperamentally we are two very different people, much too far apart in the basic things of life that make for permanence. I'm fond of you, Starr. I always have been and always will be fond of you. But it stops there."

"Only fond? That's an empty canteen for a thirsty man!" A pull of streaked bitterness lay in the words.

"For which I am so truly sorry," Julie murmured. "But it is the best I can do. . . ."

Jennette looked down at the gun at his side. "Because of this? If so, I'll throw it away!"

Again Julie shook her head. "The gun is the

least of it. And without it, you simply wouldn't be you. No, Starr — it isn't the gun."

He straightened in his saddle, drew a deep breath, lips twisting. "Well, I asked because I had to know. However, the run of events has been known to bring about changes. While you've been away, Julie — and without tough old Buck Christiansen around to keep the animals in line — many things have changed, as you'll find out. A lot of things are not as they were."

"Facts I'm prepared to face," Julie told him steadily.

"I have to wonder if you are," Jennette argued. "You got a riding boss on your hands who is running wild. That affair in town last night is only part of your outfit's new style. In the past couple of months your riding boss and crew have burned out Poe Darby and Andy Quider. They burned out Shep Riley before they killed him. Hollis Ward, being along in years and full of an old man's fears, is ready to cut and run. So far they haven't hit at me too much, probably because of this." He patted the gun at his hip.

"Yes," he went on, "Turk Roderick is traveling hog wild. Just as though he aimed to someday own Rolling C, and so is shoving everybody else out of the picture. Julie, girl — you'll have your hands more than full, trying to control that fellow!"

Julie's head came up. "I've already taken care

98

of Mister Turk Roderick. I fired him this morning. He no longer rides for me and won't, ever again!"

Starr Jennette's glance sharpened. "You mean that? And he took it?"

Julie hesitated slightly. "Not entirely. Before rushing off he said something about talking matters over again. Which will do him no good at all. Fired he is — fired he will remain!"

Jennette wagged his head from side to side, smiling faintly. "Girl, you sure have changed. I hope you can make those cards stand up. In that, you may need help. In which case you may still find use for such as Starr Jennette with his gun. Should things turn out that way, let me know. I'll still be around. Now I'll get out of your way."

He reined his horse aside and without a backward look, rode off into the sage.

For some time Julie Christiansen held her restless team in check as she watched Starr Jennette's dwindling figure, her glance darkened with the shadow of regret. In saying that she was fond of him, she had told the truth. In saying her feeling toward him could never be more than that, she again told the truth. And while fondness was fondness, it was a long way from the deeper sentiments of affection.

The man was darkly handsome and was a good companion; ever-thoughtful and considerate of her. But behind those dark eyes and features there crouched a hawkish wildness, carefully held in check, yet ever ready to blaze and fiercely destroy. A wildness that would never be directed at her, of course, yet still no thing of comfort to have hovering around or living with.

She had encountered some of the same thing in her father. In Buckley Christiansen had lain that same suggestion of couched and waiting wildness that she had feared and known anxiety over. And, she mused, it had been this kinship in makeup and character that had made Starr Jennette one of her father's favorites.

Had she, Julie brooded, been unnecessarily abrupt and blunt with that man riding way out yonder? Couldn't it have been handled in a gentler manner? Thinking that way about it, she shook her head. In matters of this sort, there was no gentler way. Because it was something that either was or was not — strictly a matter of yes or no. So now it was over and done with — another crisis met and disposed of.

Far out in the sage, Starr Jennette finally turned to look back, marking how small the buckboard and its occupant appeared against the majesty of the rim. He spoke in a murmur, a thread of wistfulness turning his tone very soft.

"Well, that's that. As always, she was strictly honest. And I wish her the best of everything! . . ."

Putting his horse into movement again, he added, "That's the way the odds run. Somebody wins — somebody loses!"

CHAPTER VI

The shadows of early evening were flooding off the rim when Orde Fraser rode into Humboldt City and hauled up at the livery barn. Nothing, he thought, so gentled a man's surroundings and made them friendly as did the smoke-blue shades of first twilight. Here, too, they softened the grim face of the rim while adding a hint of mystery that beckoned a man to go see what lay beyond.

As he stepped down and began unsaddling, Benny Rust came shuffling up to make a leading observation. "That's a pretty good bronc I sold you."

"For a fact," Fraser agreed. "Got my money's worth. And as he'll be working again tomorrow, he's earned a night of good food and care."

"Can do," Benny nodded. Ever the alert businessman, he added, "Cost you a mite."

A small grin quirked Fraser's lips. "Fair enough. Something more. I'll need a packhorse tomorrow. Got one to rent?"

"Can do," said Benny again, taking over the dun.

Orde Fraser went along to the store, there telling off a generous list of supplies. The final item brought an exclamation from Wash Butterfield.

"Six boxes of forty-fours! You aiming to start a war?"

"Not if I can help it," Fraser denied. "Poe Darby suggested the ammunition."

"Ha!" Butterfield snorted. "Poe Darby, eh? Now there is one raunchy old barbarian. You got him on your side, you're in luck. How did you manage it?"

"Met up with him at Shoshone Lake. Had a talk and decided we could get along. I'll be after this stuff early tomorrow morning. Any late news?"

"Some," Butterfield said briefly. "We laid Shep Riley away this afternoon. And this morning Julie Christiansen fired her riding boss, Turk Roderick."

Fraser was startled. "No! What brought that about?"

Butterfield hunched his high shoulders. "Considering the sort of arrogant, overbearing brute he's turned out to be, it could have been any number of things. Last night's affair was probably the final straw."

"Understandable," Fraser commented soberly. "Rough enough deal for a man to try and forget, let alone the effect it would have on a fine, gentle girl. No mail yet, of course?"

"Not until tomorrow. It's a two-day round trip out to Iron Mountain and back for Bill Weeks and his stage."

Fraser faked a shudder. "What a drive! Wears

me out just to think of it. Man must be all raw-hide and steel wire to face such a grind day-in and day-out!"

Wash Butterfield chuckled. "Save your concern. The box of that old Concord is a throne to Bill Weeks. When he's up there with the reins of a team of six in his hands, he's a king. Take him off it, he'd wither and blow away."

From the store, Fraser headed for Dan Larkin's office, hoping to find the marshal there. Which he did. Larkin was hunched over his desk, sucking on a rancid old pipe while pawing through a stack of old reward dodgers. Greeting was a brief growl.

"Been wondering about you and that Shoshone Lake range. What did you think of it?"

"Good country," Fraser said, straddling a chair. "Easy to understand why it's been fought over."

Larkin grunted. "And likely to be again."

"Not if I can avoid it," Fraser stated. "Now what's this I hear of Miss Christiansen firing that fellow, Roderick?"

Larkin leaned back in his chair, hands folded behind his head. "She had it out with him this morning, aiming to fire him. Whether he will believe her or not is something else again. Should Roderick turn stubborn, what's she to do? While her father lived, Julie had little to say about ranch affairs. Now everything is on her shoulders. Young shoulders — and alone. Makes it tough."

"Still and all, it's her ranch," Fraser argued.

"And her right to hire or fire as she pleases. Should Roderick come up mean, she can always turn to the law."

"What law?" scoffed Larkin. "Inside this town I stand for law of a sort. Take me a foot outside it, I don't rate a damn. The kind of law you're thinking of is so far away beyond the rim, you might say it doesn't exist at all. So Roderick can make it just about as mean for Julie as he pleases. And from how he looked and acted when I turned him loose, that's about the way it will be."

Orde Fraser frowned through a thoughtful moment or two, a pause broken by the hotel supper gong rolling its mellow summons across the town. He got to his feet and turned to the door, speaking quietly.

"Strikes me that somebody will have to back that fellow Roderick up against a wall and cut him down to size!"

"Somebody should," Larkin agreed. "Be a day to look forward to." He laid aside his pipe and followed Fraser out. "Last night you fed me. Tonight, I buy."

At the hotel Fraser tapped the gun at his hip. "Can't appear in Nell Viney's dining room with this thing on me. Wouldn't be decent. Besides, I can stand some soap and water. Be with you in a couple of minutes."

In his room he shucked belt and gun, had a wash, combed his damp hair with his fingers and descended to the dining room. Dan Larkin was at the same table they used the night before. When Fraser took his chair, Nell Viney brought their suppers and eyed them both severely.

"Mad at you," she told Dan Larkin. "You let that animal, Turk Roderick, out too soon. Should have kept him locked up for months and months. Now he'll make life miserable for Julie Christiansen, poor girl!"

"How's that?" Larkin demanded.

"Like this. You didn't hear what went on in my parlor today. But I did, because I made it a point to listen. In this hotel I know just where to be listening if I want to know what's going on. So I heard what Julie said and I heard what Roderick said. When she told him he was all through out at Rolling C, he came right back, rough and mean, saying she didn't know what she was talking about. After which he stamped out. So how can that lone girl get rid of him if he refuses to leave? Answer me that, Dan Larkin! And when are some of you men going to move in and help her?"

Before the badgered marshal could think up an answer, she fired the next broadside at Orde Fraser. "That goes for you too, mister. You back away and leave that girl alone. She's got troubles enough without you pestering her over your old Shoshone Lake range. You hear me — both of you!"

At this point Dan Larkin finally managed speech. "Now — now, Nell, don't be so confounded scratchy! Seeing you're telling us what to do, I'll tell you what you should do. Which is go out to Rolling C headquarters for a few days and give Julie your moral support. Be good for her and good for you. You've been cooped up in this hotel so long without a break, you've got cabin fever. The Indian girls can handle things for a week without you around."

Nell Viney's mood quieted a little. "I may do just that. I may have Benny Rust drive me out. At the same time, the pair of you mind what I say!"

She marched off, head high. Grim amusement crinkled Dan Larkin's eye corners as his glance followed her.

"Mighty fine woman, Nellie is," he rumbled softly. "You hear a lot about the brave breed of men who tamed the west. Don't ever forget the brave breed of women who were there, too, sharing all the dangers and the hardships. Over the long haul it's frankly my feeling that the women were the ones who really tamed it. And there goes one of them."

Supper done, Larkin brought out a cigar, sniffed it with keen relish, then lit up, mouthing the first drag of smoke luxuriously. "Ain't often I make out with one of these. Pete Eagle gave it to me. His way of saying thanks for cooling Turk Roderick down last night. The pure quill, Pete is — one of our best citizens. Sorry I haven't another of these for you."

Already spinning up a Durham smoke,

Fraser grinned. "Obliged, but this is more my speed. Now I'm off for a look at the street, and I'm leaving my gun in my room. What do you think?"

Cigar alight and drawing well, Dan Larkin displayed a vast content. "Should be safe enough. No hostiles around just now. Nights hereabouts are not all like the last one. Most generally, things are quiet and mild enough. Just the same, keep that wary eye on your back trail."

On the hotel porch, Fraser found a chair and settled back to watch the night come fully down. Massive against the first glitter of stars, the rim was a black and brooding presence. A small shift of air, sliding down from that lofty crest, brought with it the breath of pine and cedar, together with the luring hint of a complete wildness. Still on hand, last night's screech owl mewed fretfully in the cottonwoods.

Trailing cigar smoke, Dan Larkin made a leisurely way down to Butterfield's store. Down that way also, the lights of Pete Eagle's Ten High Bar peered out with yellow eyes.

While noting these several things idly, Orde Fraser's thoughts skimmed back over the past score of days, raking up the highlights of those days. Like the talk he'd had with L. J. Blackwell in the latter's Winnemucca bank office. Long Les Blackwell, as Henry Greer had referred to him, using the tag somewhat slightingly, as though from animosity.

Which, Fraser mused, didn't amount to a damn. No matter what Henry Greer thought, the fact remained that Lester Blackwell had sure treated him fair and well, going to the time and expense of seeking him out as Yance Milliken's lone heir, all of which translated to a rich inheritance. In addition, the Winnemucca banker stood ready to back him financially and aid him in starting a herd of his own. Certainly, nothing could have been more generous. . . .

Taking a final pull at his cigarette, Fraser flipped the butt out into the street's dust and watched the crimson spark of it fade quickly to nothingness. All things concerned, he decided wryly, the abrupt change in his personal fortunes was a little overwhelming. From pounding a saddle as Toby Whipple's riding boss, to ownership of a big chunk of prime range, plus the further promise of ending up as a full-fledged cattleman in his own right; it was enough to set any man back on his heels with wonderment.

Came now the scuff of dust-muffled hoofs as a single rider jogged into sight and hauled up at Wash Butterfield's hitch rack — there to get down, tie, and move into the store. A few moments later the rider emerged and came plodding up street toward the hotel. From his place in the deep shadow, Orde Fraser watched this approach warily. The new arrival climbed the steps and sent his call forward, tentative and uncertain.

"Mister Fraser? I am Hollis Ward. I'd like a word with you if that is agreeable. Dan Larkin said I'd probably find you here."

There was no hint of threat or hostility in the words; rather a meek, almost apologetic note. Fraser answered readily.

"Of course. Drag up a chair."

The man made a slight, shrunken figure, sighing tiredly as he took his seat with weary complaint.

"Years sure take it out of a man. Time was when I could fork saddle leather from dawn and never think a thing about it. But no more! Just the jog from home to town tuckers me now. You don't mind me taking some of your time?"

"Not at all, Mr. Ward. The night's young."

Still for a moment, Hollis Ward cleared his throat. "Poe Darby was by my place this evening with word about you and the Shoshone Lake range. I got a fair scatter of beef on that grass, using it like everybody else has done. Poe says you own that range now, so I'll get my stuff off as quick as I can, with no hard feelings either way. Wanted you to know that."

"Fair enough," Orde Fraser assured him. "No need to rush about your stock, either. I've got plenty of time, while wanting trouble no more than you do."

"That," said Hollis Ward, "makes for good listening. Quarreling over range can be bad business. Most generally, everybody loses

109

something somewhere. I've been up and down the cattle trails for a lot of years and never gained anything permanent myself or saw anybody else do it by mixing rough in range trouble. Just the same, friend, I'm afraid you got a real quarrel ahead of you."

"Meaning Rolling C?" Fraser murmured.

Hollis Ward bobbed his head. "Buck Christiansen was a rough old cob, but by and large he played it pretty fair and square. You tried to take a bite out of his hide and he'd eat you alive. But you let him alone, he'd leave you alone. Yeah, I got along real good with old Buck. But this fellow, Turk Roderick — he's all out and out pirate. So you can expect trouble there."

"Seems to be the general opinion," Fraser agreed. "But that is a chore I'll handle when I come up against it."

"Given even half a chance, Roderick will push you over," Hollis Ward cautioned. "I know, because he's got me teetering right now. And take what happened to Shep Riley last night. Hadn't known about it until Poe told me. No matter what Shep might have done, it wasn't enough to deserve what they did to him."

Thinking about it the cattleman was quiet for a little time, shaking his head. Then he glanced down street where the lights of the Ten High Bar beckoned. "Generally spend a little time with my good friend Pete Eagle when I come to town. I'd admire to have you drink with me, Mr. Fraser?"

Orde Fraser got to his feet. "A privilege, Mr. Ward."

Angling down street with Hollis Ward hardly up to his shoulder, Fraser had renewed impression of a tired, discouraged old man, an impression that was heightened when they pushed through the saloon doors into the warm glow of light beyond. Alone and busy with small bar chores, Pete Eagle's black eyes sparked with pleasure at sight of Fraser's companion.

"Evening, Hollis! Good to see you again. Been quite some time — been too long since we had a drink together and a couple of games of cribbage. Things being slow just now, maybe we can make up for that?"

"By jollies, yes!" exclaimed Hollis Ward. "Was hoping it might be that way. Ain't turned a card since I was here last time. And Pete, might you have something left in that special bottle of yours?"

Under a weather-beaten, flop-brimmed old Stetson, Hollis Ward's hair was thin and white. He was a time- and toil-warped little man, worn down by the weight of long, hard years. Orde Fraser knew a swift sympathy and liking for him.

From under the bar, Pete Eagle brought up a deck of cards and a cribbage board of dark, heavy wood and laid them on the bar top.

"There they are, Hollis," he grinned. "All the

necessary tools of friendly combat. And here is that special bottle."

He set it out, together with glasses. Hollis Ward poured, showing Fraser a faded glance as he lifted his glass. "Friend, your good health and success. Pete, shuffle the cards!"

They drank and put their glasses down. At that moment, hoofs came to a trampling halt outside in the street as a rider fought his mount with a flurry of curses. Spur chains dragged, the door of the saloon kicked open, and the new arrival swaggered in. Hollis Ward's exclamation was small and dismayed.

"Rube Yard! It would have to be somebody like him!"

Hulking and truculent, the rider looked over the room and the people in it. His eyes were muddy and deep-set. As he identified Orde Fraser and the little man beside him, a swift satisfaction livened his glance. He showed the purpose behind his thinking immediately by moving up and jamming a hard shoulder into Hollis Ward, driving the old man against the bar while lashing him with rough and ruthless words.

"What you doing here, you worthless old dog? You've been told to stay out of town, to crawl off somewhere and die, making room for a better man. Also told what to expect if you didn't listen. Here's some of it! . . ."

Emphasis for this was an open-handed slap in the face that bruised Hollis Ward's mouth and spun him half around.

Missing no part of Rube Yard's first calculating survey of the room, Orde Fraser immediately guessed the scheme that was building in this fellow's feral mind. Yard's real objective reached a good deal farther than the mistreatment of Hollis Ward. What Rube Yard was out to do was drag Fraser himself into an argument. For he had no gun with him, while Rube had one on his hip. Plainly, this was what lay behind Rube Yard's scheming.

In wanting to move peacefully into the workings of this stretch of country, Orde Fraser thought he had successfully laid and tamped down the fires of hot anger that had gusted so fiercely over last night's happenings. He found now that he hadn't. Those fires had merely been banked and so now they burst forth again in a bitterly consuming flame.

Because here again was more of the calculated, ruthless overplay that had driven him down into the dust beside the stage and was set to maul him mercilessly with the advantage of heavy odds. Here again was the same feral brutality that had dragged Shep Riley to ignominious, savage death and more of the same, dark treachery in the one who had tried to gun him down as he stood on the porch of Wash Butterfield's store.

Beyond the bar, Pete Eagle had come up on his toes, a growl of angry protest forming in his throat. But Fraser got into bitter action ahead

113

of him. A swift sweep of one arm lifted Hollis Ward out of the way, his free hand sliding along the bar and coming up clutching the heavy cribbage board. And with this he belted Rube Yard savagely across the face.

It was a wicked, destroying blow — and meant to be that way — with the cribbage board splintering at the impact. A man of lesser physical bulk than Rube Yard would have been knocked flat. Even so, though thick and burly, with the heavy bones and insensitivity to punishment of some prowling brute; Rube Yard went reeling back, dazed and floundering. A gout of crimson leaped to fan down over his mouth and chin and, with the muddy depths of his eyes blurred from shock, he fumbled for his gun.

Alert to such a move, Fraser dropped the shattered remains of the cribbage board, jerked the gun from Rube's near-flaccid grasp and tossed the weapon aside. After which, laughing bleakly, he went for Rube with slashing, hammering fists, driving him back into a poker table that skidded wildly under the press of Rube's floundering weight.

Animal-strong as he was, Rube Yard never fully recovered from the smashing impact of the splintered cribbage board. He swung blindly and uselessly at Fraser a time or two, and in between swings kept grabbing at his empty holster as though unable to realize that no gun was there. It was the unconscious reaction of one to whom possession of a gun was his only real moral strength. With it he might be a vicious, coldblooded killer; but without it, he was just a numbed and clumsy clod.

Keeping his man backed against the table, Orde Fraser set out to destroy him with battering, merciless fists. He was still working at this resolve when Dan Larkin's gruff growl cut through the dark ferocity that convulsed him.

"About enough now I think, friend Fraser. Unless you really aim to kill him. But if you're just out to prove a point, I'd say off-hand that you can consider it done. The only thing holding him up is the table."

From the doorway of Butterfield's store the marshal had watched Rube Yard haul up at the Ten High and swagger in, so he had crossed over to see what was what. He arrived just in time to see Orde Fraser swing the cribbage board and get rid of Rube Yard's gun. Then for a little time he had watched subsequent proceedings with an observant and not entirely unappreciative eye. However, with the business of the star designating certain duties, he had then moved in to restore the peace.

Fraser backed away reluctantly. He scrubbed a palm across his jaw where one of Rube Yard's pawing swings had touched. And he spoke his feelings harshly.

"This damned country! I've told people to leave me alone. Maybe I'll have to kill somebody before they understand that I mean what I say!"

"Quite so — quite so!" Larkin soothed. Dry amusement quirked his lips as he eyed Rube Yard's sagging figure. "What started the fuss?"

"My fault, Dan," said Hollis Ward quickly. "Soon as Yard showed up he started to rawhide me and push me around. Friend Fraser wouldn't stand for that. Reckon I shouldn't have come to town. Yeah, Dan — all my fault. If I hadn't been here, nothing would have happened."

"There you're wrong," Fraser countered. "I was the turkey Yard was after. Minute he saw I didn't have a gun on me, he started trouble — hoping probably to push things far enough to rack up a cheap kill. And without a gun, all I could do was use the cribbage board on him." He looked across the bar at Pete Eagle. "I'm sorry about your cribbage board, Pete."

"Don't you be," said Pete quickly. "Never saw a cribbage board used to better effect. Dan, it all happened just the way you heard. Now run that fellow Yard out of here before I take on where Fraser left off!"

Grinning, the marshal took Yard by the arm and hustled him toward the door. "You hear that, Rube? This is no place for you. Should you hang around this spot, the sky might fall on you. So you get back to where you came from. And be sure you tell Turk Roderick what happened — and why!"

Rube Yard offered neither answer nor objection. Groggy and stupid from the going over he'd absorbed, he shambled heavily out ahead of the marshal. As the door closed, Hollis Ward turned to Orde Fraser worriedly.

"Mighty sorry about this. Never would want to see trouble come your way on my account. I should have stayed away from town."

"Nothing of the sort, Hollis," put in Pete Eagle. "You got as much right in town as any other man. And always more than welcome in this place. I agree with Fraser. He was the one Yard was after. He just used you to get trouble started."

Outside sounded the mutter of departing hoofs along the street, and the saloon doors winnowed under the push of Dan Larkin's return. He was alternately grinning and chuckling aloud.

"Departing from our midst goes one sick hombre — one mighty sick hombre. What with his nose bent crooked, some teeth knocked out, plus a lot of sore and aching spots, I'd say friend Rube is in for a damn rough night. I doubt he'll get much sleep." Crossing to a far corner, Larkin picked up Rube Yard's gun. "I'll take care of this, Pete, should he ever come looking for it."

Nodding, Pete put a fresh bottle on the bar. "Now a friendly one, just between the four of us."

Shortly after that, Orde Fraser left for the hotel and bed. Pete Eagle's approving glance followed him. "One of the quiet ones, Dan. That's it — quiet! But when they get started — Lordy! ..."

Dan Larkin chuckled. "I've heard it said that all tigers walk softly. Could be something to that."

Climbing to his room, Orde Fraser knew the drag of weariness. In part, it was a physical thing; in part, mental. More than either, perhaps — the aftermath of explosive action.

Stripped, he had a good wash, then lay back on his bed in the soft, warm dark. The room was a refuge. In it now, as in the night beyond his open window, lay peace and quiet. Also, within himself, a quietness was taking over. Harsh action had released all the blazing anger and explosive pressures. It was as he had discovered on occasion along the back trail. Once a spell of the old red rage had burned out, it left a man feeling strangely clean and content.

CHAPTER VII

When Buckley Christiansen built Rolling C headquarters, he did so with three requisites in mind — utility, longevity and authority. In particular, the authority a man could feel when looking out over a quarter million acres of his own land. So the spot finally selected was on an elevated benchland tucked up under the dark and towering flank of the Humboldt Rim.

Fashioned to endure in a harsh and wild land, the stone-built ranch house lay long and low with a deep porch all across the front of it. On this porch beside the heavily planked front door stood an ancient armchair, seated and backed with parchment-hard rawhide, worn smooth and shiny from years of use.

During his declining years Buck Christiansen spent many hours in that chair; while from under shaggy, grizzled brows the hard-shelled old cattleman measured the worth of this range he had fashioned for his own, together with the shifting tides of cattle that crossed and recrossed it.

Planted by his own hands, the tapered green of poplar trees framed and shaded Buck Christiansen's home. Farther back beyond a generous interval stood the other ranch structures; the bunkhouse with its connecting cook shack, the barns and feed sheds. Past these, at the very base of the rim, sprawled the several corrals.

Here, too, the face of the rim was deep-cut by a wye-shaped gorge; each arm of which fed generous and never-failing spring water into a single, alder-shaded stream that flowed past headquarters and lost itself in the long-running miles of the range below for the benefit of the cattle roaming it. Such was the seat of Buckley Christiansen's cattle kingdom and the home Julie Christiansen looked up to while covering the last dusty reaches of the road leading to it.

Home, she thought — home! Home and all the responsibilities once fled from, but now returned to . . . with eagerness! . . .

Here the road began to tilt upward and the buckboard team slowed to a walk, leaning heavily into the pull. How well-remembered this short stretch of steepness; how, as a little girl, she had loved to race down it with eyes shining and her hair flying, to greet her father on his return from town with a wagon load of supplies. He would reach down a big, strong hand to swing her lightly up beside him. Nearly always he would have a surprise for her; a trinket of some sort dear to a little girl's heart, or a bag of hard candy from the big glass jar on Wash Butterfield's store counter.

In those days a very close bond had existed between father and daughter, but one that had begun to erode and weaken as Julie grew older. This was a thing she had done a great deal of thinking about before coming to understand the why of it. With the years closing in on him, Buck Christiansen's concern for the future of his hard-won ranch holdings had steadily deepened, and with it a reluctance to leave that future in the hands of a lone, stripling girl.

At one time Julie had reasoned with some bitterness that had she been boy instead of girl, things might have been different. For apparently, to old Buck's rough and fundamental way of thinking, only a man could properly handle a man's job. Ridden by this deep conviction he had to some degree moved away from her. But later, when Julie came to understand how her father's judgement had been swayed by his strong sense of possession, the bitterness went away. She knew then that he was merely doing what he thought would best guarantee the security of those possessions for her future benefit. However, he had not lived to witness the real results of this reasoning; so now the entire problem was hers and hers alone! It was a hand she had to play by herself.

With distance shortening, Julie's eagerness increased and her searching glance reached for glimpses of all the well-remembered things. Like the chair by the front door, and the trace of color where the Cherokee rose climbed a corner post of the porch — the rose planted and nursed and dearly loved by the mother she had lost so long, long ago. An image of beauty and gentleness she could barely recall. It was like trying to bring back a shadow out of the distant past. . . .

Then there was the iron hitch rail between two of the poplar trees, and when Julie put the sorrels up to this, set the brake and climbed down, her glance went across the interval to the bunkhouse. Lounging there in the doorway was the only ranch hand in sight. With some show of reluctance he flipped a cigarette butt aside and came sauntering. He was one whom Julie had never seen before and when he spoke, there was a careless insolence behind his words.

"Want I should take care of the team?"

"What else?" Julie met curtness with curtness. "Grain them, then have them taken back to town."

The fellow made no move toward helping with the luggage, leaving her to wrestle it onto the porch by herself. It was an open discourtesy that fostered both an edge of anger and a brittle question.

"What's your name?"

Smiling thinly, the puncher tipped a shoulder. "Bartle, ma'am — Cass Bartle. Why you ask?"

"So I'll know it when I decide to write out your time!"

She left it that way and got her gear inside, where she found little change save the inevitable musty atmosphere of forlorn emptiness peculiar to a house left untenanted for any length of time. Fighting this sense of isolation, she moved quickly about opening doors and windows, letting in the day's warm, space-scented breath.

Her own room was exactly as she had left it, the bed carelessly made up. Sight of this disarray aroused a half-shamed memory of the morning when she had left so hurriedly; at the time not at all sure she would ever return. Yet return she had, and with so many things to do she got right at them, stripping the blankets from the bed, shaking them out and spreading them over chairs to air and sweeten.

Her father's room was next. Spartan plain, it held only what old Buck thought was really necessary for any man's needs. On a wall peg hung his favorite coat, a time-honored sheepskin with badly frayed sleeve ends and the collar fleece worn down to nothing. Bleached and stained by sun and storm and long, hard usage, scorched in several places by errant branding fire embers; it bespoke more than any other one thing the father Julie Christiansen remembered. A lump formed in her throat and her eyes misted. Stirred with sudden feeling she lifted the garment down and hugged it briefly.

Even more of a man's hangout was the ranch office. A big room, this was the real heart of the Rolling C cattle empire. Here, down across the years, the fortunes of the ranch, good and bad, had been discussed and resolved. Here, in clouds of tobacco smoke and over toddies based on some of Pete Eagle's best bourbon whiskey, owner and hired hands had worked out countless ranch problems. Also, in this room right now, lay evidence of recent occupancy.

On one corner of the heavy oaken table that served as a desk, several use-scummed glasses and a bottle of whiskey stood. On another, there was the tin lid of a lard pail piled high with the butts of brown paper cigarettes. Several badly thumbed tally and time books were scattered about together with numerous scraps of paper covered with the scrawl of written figures.

Turk Roderick, of course, Julie reasoned. Turk Roderick moved in and took over as though he owned the place!

The big, black-iron heating stove stood cold now. But how well-remembered were the winter nights when the snow lay thick on the outside world and she would curl up in the old easy chair beside the stove and bask kitten-like in the glowing warmth while her father worked at his desk.

Shelves filled one wall. On another were racked two rifles, old Buck's favorite British-made shotgun and a holstered six-shooter with its cartridge belt — the plain walnut grip of the big Colt gun stained dark with age and use. How momentous the day when, at her father's insistence, she first fired a shot from the heavy Peacemaker! Even though using both hands, she barely held on as the gun rumbled with re-port and fought back with recoil.

But old Buck had kept her practicing with it until she learned to handle it reasonably well. It was a gun kept always loaded, her father vowing that a gun was made to shoot with, and if unloaded, was only a partially useful club. It was loaded now and, as Julie hefted the solid weight of it, she became soberly thoughtful, considering the cold, hard facts of the present, and uncomfortably aware of how, in so many ways, she was completely alone.

Next stop was the ranch kitchen. Together with her personal luggage, Julie had brought a week's supply of groceries from Wash Butterfield's store. These she sorted and stored on the kitchen shelves. Here, too, she saw evi-dence of recent use. The woodbox and the water bucket were full, a fact she wondered at, but accepted. And now, more to be doing something than because of any hunger, she fired up the stove, put on a pot of coffee and fashioned a simple meal.

While eating, she watched from the window at her elbow for some sign of the usual ranch activity at this time of day. But, aside from the buckboard team tied at the corral fence, and a scatter of other horses in the corral beyond, no life showed anywhere. At a glance the place ap-peared deserted, but Julie knew perfectly well that this was not so, as the saddle pole beside the cavvy corral gate was lined with riding gear.

Also, a thin seep of smoke eddied above the cook shack chimney.

This, she decided, would all be Turk Roderick's doing, his way of showing the weight of his authority. He had the crew holed up, waiting for her to weaken and make some sort of advance; a conclusion that angered Julie, yet dismayed her, too. She had told the man that he was through, and this was his way of proving her wrong. As Henry Greer had warned, it would not be easy, getting rid of Turk Roderick!

Fretting with impatience, Julie found that time could move very slowly. And there must be no weakening on her part. She had made and declared her decision and there must be no slight sign of backing away from it. If Turk Roderick wanted to make this a waiting game, so be it. One factor was to her advantage: it was not in Turk Roderick's makeup to be passive. Intolerant of resistance of any sort, the man was too arrogant, too rough-shod, too sure of himself in all ways to accept a stalemate. Sooner or later he would try to smash through any obstacle that thwarted him.

To use some of that slow-moving time, Julie busied herself about the house; sweeping, dusting, making up her bed, unpacking and sorting out her luggage. Again and again as the afternoon wore away she looked from the kitchen window, hoping to note some change in the outside scene, but finding none.

It was almost sinister, the way things remained so empty of human activity or movement. Almost as though the ranch had died, Julie mused morbidly. But sundown came finally and, with it, the first change. A burly ranch hand left the bunkhouse and crossed to the cavvy corral. Here he caught and saddled, then tied the mount behind the buckboard before getting into the rig and driving away in the direction of town.

With the arrival of full dark, the house seemed more empty than ever, and the outside world more somber and threatening. Came now the first threads of panic. Huddled in the kitchen, Julie was angry with herself over this show of weakness, this feeling of insecurity and all other such useless fears. These four walls now sheltering her and the long-reaching miles of range land all round about were hers, and hers alone. And only she, Julie Christiansen, could and would make that claim. . . .

So, presently, there was the warm glow of lamplight and a cup of hot coffee to comfort her and bring back her confidence. Now, also, lamplight gleamed in the windows of the bunkhouse and the cook shack. Julie opened the kitchen window so that she might listen as well as look. All that came through to her was the great, wild silence of space flowing down from the crest of the rim. She carried the lamp into the office and there began going through all the papers on the desk in an effort to fix her mind on something besides the sly, creeping figments of uncertainty.

After a considerable and useless time of this, she lifted the big Colt gun from its holster and carried both it and the lamp into her room. Here, she tucked the gun under her pillow and made ready for the night. Tired though she was, sleep evaded her and it was long after before the mutter of approaching hoofs came to her out of the night. Listening intently, she heard this traveler move past the house and cross the interval to the corrals.

And in some strange way, as though this arrival had put a period to the day, Julie Christiansen was able to finally relax and drift off to sleep.

In town, Orde Fraser greeted the new day while the stars were still high and bright and the rim a solid wall of blackness. He dressed, washed up and moved downstairs to the hotel kitchen where the Indian girls were already busy under lamplight preparing for breakfast. One of them showed him a shy smile and pointed to a table in the corner. She was pouring his coffee when Nell Viney came in, dressed for travel.

"Got your nerve," she scolded mildly. "Nobody but the owner and the hired help eat in this kitchen."

Orde Fraser grinned. "Just wanting to make the least trouble possible. Now the owner of this place can eat with me. You look like you're aiming to go somewhere?"

"Rolling C," Nell Viney said, sniffing the coffee fragrance. "Told you and Dan Larkin so last night." She eyed him intently, then laid a fingertip along the angle of his jaw. "More signs of combat. Who with this time?"

"Rube Yard. A trouble hunter."

"Worse!" declared Nell Viney flatly. "A foul animal. I hope you beat his filthy ears off. Times like this I could grow real fond of you, Orde Fraser."

They ate in silence. When Fraser built a cigarette and rose to leave, Nell Viney looked up. "Tell Benny Rust he's driving me out to Rolling C — probably for all day. And you," she added soberly, "you be careful. Because Rube Yard is just the sort to lay out with a rifle hoping for a shot at you — preferably at your back!"

"Thought of that," Fraser nodded. "More and more I'm running scared. But," he added, with a dry twinkle, "not too scared."

Outside, dawn was quickening, the town coming awake. Wash Butterfield was open for business, with Fraser's order of supplies piled on the store porch. Lantern light shone palely in the runway of the livery stable, where Benny Rust waited with the dun and a pack animal. Both horses were saddled and ready for travel.

"Figgered you'd likely be ridin' early," Benny explained. "And use of the pack bronc ain't costin' you a cent."

Startled, Fraser asked, "How so? I'm not asking for favors."

"Ain't no favor," Benny shrugged. "Just payin' off a debt kinda left-handed like."

Fraser measured the rotund little livery owner in the thin lantern light. "Benny, you sure you're sober?"

Benny chuckled. "Stone cold. Now here's how it is. I understand that last night you walloped the supreme hell out of Rube Yard?"

"There was a little ruckus, yes. What's that got to do with it?"

"Plenty!" Benny emphasized. "Wish I could have done it. But I'm no fist-fightin' man — ain't built right for it. Now more'n once Rube's throwed his weight at me. Fact is, when he brought my sorrel team and buckboard back from Rolling C last night, he slapped me around some, for no good reason except plain damn meanness. Now mebbe I am just a fat old busted-down stable roustabout, but I got feelin's and a smidgin of pride, same as other folks. So when I heard of the goin' over you gave him, I felt good. I felt real good! Even made me sleep good, too. So should you try to pay me for the hire of this pack bronc, you'd be hurtin' my feelin's."

Fraser dropped a hand on Benny's plump shoulder. "That's the way you want it, my friend — that's the way it will be. But when dealing with such as Rube Yard, you should keep a gun handy, and use it if you have to.

Now here's a word from Nell Viney. You're to drive her out to Rolling C, probably for the day."

Full morning surged up over the eastern edge of the world as Orde Fraser left Humboldt City — the dun at a fast, swinging walk, the packhorse shuffling at lead behind. Peering into the sun's flat rays, Fraser pulled his hat low. Shadow of rider and horses stretched long behind and under the blaze of the sun. Last night's coolness was soon wiped out by the raw flavor of warming sage.

Keep an eye on your back trail, Dan Larkin had warned. In relation to Rube Yard, Nell Viney had offered similar advice. Considering this, Fraser decided there was little immediate danger from Rube Yard. Just the same, he kept a searching glance swinging. So it was that out some considerable distance ahead he picked up a stir of movement that became a rider, hauled up now and waiting in the trail.

The rider had made no attempt at concealment which pretty well denied any hostile attempt, so Fraser closed in confidently. At closer range, recognition came and he lifted a hand in greeting as he eyed Starr Jennette with some wonderment. Jennette showed the edge of a tired smile as he swung his mount into step with the dun.

"Figured you'd be riding this way, so waited out for you."

Fraser's glance narrowed. "Waited out? You mean all night?"

Nodding, Jennette scrubbed a hand across a whisker-roughened jaw. "Made a siwash camp of it. Wanted a talk."

For some time they rode in silence, Jennette staring straight ahead. He showed the effects of that hardship camp; his shoulders humped, his head hanging a little. Long hours of little sleep could do that to a man and Orde Fraser wondered why the need.

Abruptly Jennette straightened and laid out a flat, bluntly taut question. "Just how far do you figure to go with this Shoshone Lake deal?"

Glance swinging, Fraser shifted in his saddle. "Only far enough to claim what is legitimately mine. Would you be thinking otherwise?"

"Maybe."

"On account of something Turk Roderick might have said?"

Jennette's laugh was short and harsh. "Never would believe anything that fellow said — ever! No, this is some whiskey talk I heard over at Hayfork Crossing."

"Hayfork Crossing — where's that?"

"Over east a piece. Used to be a stage stop between here and the Owyhee country. But when the railroad built into Iron Mountain, it pulled all the trade and travel that way and Hayfork Crossing pretty much faded out. Nothing there now but three, four old buildings that make up a bar, an eating place and some sleeping quarters of sorts. Swede Soderman owns and runs the layout. Now and then I drift over that way, just to be going somewhere."

"And that's where you heard this whiskey talk?" Fraser probed. "Was it something about me?"

Jennette twisted up and lit a Durham cigarette before answering. When he did it was another abrupt, curt question. "You know Fitch Carlin?"

"Heard of him, but never met him," Fraser said. "What about him?"

"He's putting a herd together over in the Owyhee country and pointing it this way. A couple of stray punchers at Swede Soderman's bar were talking it over. They had tried to sign on with Carlin, but he had a full crew already. And now, if you didn't know it, Fitch Carlin is the big, bad wolf of some Winnemucca banker who owns cow outfits all across three states. And according to the general word, when Fitch Carlin heads into new country with a big herd, somebody in that country ends up minus their range. So — the question in my mind runs like this — where is that Carlin herd going to end up?"

"That," Fraser explained, "is easy answered. I'm expecting some cattle brought in to stock my Shoshone Lake range. Not a real big herd, though. Maybe about five hundred head."

"Way the Hayfork talk went, Carlin's herd is four, five times that much."

"Then what you heard was whiskey talk and nothing else," said Fraser bluntly. "No herd

133

that size is slated for my range. And nobody runs cattle on it without my permission."

"Including me?" Jennette murmured.

Again Fraser twisted in his saddle, meeting Jennette's dark glance straight on. "Yes — including you."

Jennette smiled faintly. "Been disappointed if you'd said different. And it's all right with me, because I'm on my way out and want it so. Right now my brand amounts to very little, maybe a hundred and fifty head. I've come to realize I never was cut out to be a real cattleman in my own right. Can't seem to settle down and stay put. So I'm making you a proposition. Any stuff of mine you run across, vent to your own iron and pay me later at the going feeder price. A deal?"

"If I said yes, it wouldn't be fair to you," Fraser argued. "Feeder price wouldn't be enough."

"Would for me," shrugged Jennette. "I'm not greedy and I'll always get along. I just don't want to be bothered owning anything anymore. My horse and saddle. My gun. The clothes on my back, that's enough for me. I'm making you this proposition with my eyes open, so don't feel you're taking any advantage of me."

Fraser studied him for a moment. "Very well, it's a deal. And you can take it that whatever the tally is, it will be correct."

Again the twisted, slightly bitter smile. "I'm sure it will. So that angle is off my mind. Now

134

I'll be completely footloose, free to travel to hell and back, should the idea strike. Mister, you've done me a favor, and can do me one more."

"Glad to. Name it."

Starr Jennette searched for words before speaking slowly. "It is about a lady. Miss Julie Christiansen."

Fraser's glance turned needle-sharp. "Make it careful. Because she is a lady — a very real and perfect one!"

"Which I know, even better than you," Jennette said quietly. "The other night in the hotel when I came to your door, she was in the room with you, wasn't she?"

"She was there," Fraser admitted, "more like a scared little kid than anything else. But every inch a lady — and treated as such."

"Which I also know," nodded Jennette. "If she hadn't been, you'd be dead by this time."

They let this flat statement hang while the stillness of a wide and empty world settled in, a stillness broken only by the soft creak and squeal of saddle leather and the steady mutter of hoofs churning up a thin haze of amber trail dust. It was Fraser who finally spoke.

"What I can't figure is why she should be afraid of you."

"Long story, best untold," Jennette said with careful softness. "At that time she hadn't fully made up her mind about a number of things. Now she has, which is good, because it is her life to live. Her father, old Buck Christiansen, may have meant well, but he was way wrong in trying to order something he didn't really understand, and which, with the blue chips down, was none of his business. Of course, she never had cause to be afraid of me about anything in the slightest, which she fully understands, now. So I wish her nothing but the best of everything, and I'm going to be around to see that nobody — and I mean nobody — gives her a bad deal in any way. Now, seeing we've had our little talk and set up our cattle deal, I'll shake along on my own."

They reined in, side by side, and over a long pause appraised each other intently, reading the depth of character couched behind this mutual glance. It was Jennette who finally smiled above an outstretched hand.

"Friend, I like your style. And wish you luck!"

Orde Fraser met the hand heartily. "Right back at you, brother. And should you ever get the urge to hire out your saddle again, let me know!"

CHAPTER VIII

At Rolling C headquarters, day's first light came down past the rim to stir Julie Christiansen from deep sleep. For a little time she was lazily still, eyes half-lidded, thoughts drowsy and unformed. Then came the hard impact of realization and she pushed up on one elbow, fully awake to the day and all its portents.

The house was charged with night's lingering chill, which hurried her through her dressing and into the kitchen to get a fire going. As soon as the tin basin of water was even slightly warm, she washed up and returned to her room to brush her hair and spend a moment or two before her mirror, seeking any hint of physical change to match her new mental and emotional outlook. If change there be, it showed only in the deeper color of her cheeks.

Again in the kitchen with thoughts on breakfast, she stole a look from the window, seeing at once that the inertia of yesterday was done with. Out at the corrals, men were catching and saddling. Out there also was a man named Roderick, stalking here and there and laying out orders for the day.

That man, she thought, would never change.

There was no patience or tolerance in him. And so she knew that before this day was done, she would have to again face those hostile forces and put her new-found spirit and purpose against their bullying threat. She had done so in Nell Viney's parlor, so she certainly could do no less within the four walls of her own home. The decisions of yesterday would be the decisions of today. Nor would she change! . . .

Hot coffee and breakfast strengthened the resolve and she ate hungrily. She washed the dishes, then returned to her room to make up her bed and tidy things otherwise. In doing this, she uncovered the big Colt gun she had put under her pillow last night and now knew a touch of shamed amusement at her useless fears. So now, as she went into the office she took the gun with her and returned it to its rightful place in the holster on the wall rack. After which she took the chair behind the desk to await the day's developments. This chair had been Buckley Christiansen's post of authority when he managed the destinies of the ranch. Now both the chair and the responsibilities were hers. So be it! . . .

Out at the corrals Turk Roderick watched the last of the crew scatter off on the daily business of the ranch. After which he turned and laid a long, hard stare at the ranch house, noting the drift of smoke above the kitchen chimney. His heavy jaw jutted and the lids of his eyes pinched down. He ground a clenched fist into the palm of the other hand as though he were crushing something mentally.

That little fool yonder! Who was she to think she could stand against him? What chance did she have of bossing the hard-shelled crew he'd just ordered out to their work? Why, hell! . . . They'd laugh at her and do as they damn well pleased. And when they did, what could she do about it? Oh, she'd learn, all right — she'd learn the hard way!

He would, so Roderick told himself, point out these facts when he went presently to face her. But he wouldn't go just yet. Instead, he'd give her some more silent treatment and see if she had any moves of her own to make. Yeah — let her stew a little longer! . . .

Returning to the bunkhouse he was met by a mixture of grunts, groans, and thick, mumbled curses. On a corner bunk, Rube Yard was shifting and turning. He looked a veritable gargoyle, his face all one great bruise, his nose a swollen blob, his lips pouting rolls of lacerated flesh and his eyes near-hidden by puffed, blue-black lids.

There was no slightest hint of sympathy in either Roderick's glance or his harsh words.

"Shut up! Quit that damn sniveling. You asked for your misery. Maybe you learned something by what happened to you, but I doubt it — you being so damn thick-headed!"

"What I did was for the ranch — for you," Rube Yard mumbled.

"What you did was try to run a blazer. I sent you to town last night to do two things. One was to return the team and buckboard to Rust's stable. The other was to look and listen and measure the temper of the town. But you weren't content to play it that smart. You had to start throwing your weight around and got damn well curried for it. So quit your whining and belly-aching. You'll still live to be hung!"

Rube Yard fumbled a whiskey bottle to his punished mouth, sucked at it greedily, then subsided to lesser groans and curses. Turk Roderick pulled a chair to the bunkhouse table, scrambled a deck of grimy, hard-used cards together and laid out a hand of solitaire. But soon he pushed the cards aside and sat brooding, staring straight ahead at a mind picture he had built of the future. Which was the picture of himself in the spot Buckley Christiansen had occupied. Complete master of Rolling C and all it meant in the way of power, prestige and possession.

So many times he had built such a picture and ever it grew more and more luring and de-sired. And never until the last forty-eight hours had he known any real doubt of its coming true. But now that fool girl had returned from her journeying, shaping up stiff-necked and contentious. Now, despite all previous swagger and bluster, a shred of doubt had risen to plague him.

It was the fact of her sex that had him

stumped. A man could be handled in a lot of ways — all rough. But a young woman, stubborn and opinionated, what the hell — what the hell! . . . Maybe he had played his cards wrong. Maybe if he had bowed and scraped and sweet-talked her, she'd have been willing to marry him, which would have taken care of everything. Too late now to hope for anything like that. In Nell Viney's parlor she had looked at him like he was something that had just crawled out of some dark and noisome place. Damn fool girl! . . .

Then of course that fellow Fraser had to show up, claiming the Shoshone Lake range. A tough one, that fellow — as he had proven on the evening of his arrival in Humboldt City. Further proof of that toughness was right yonder on the corner bunk, grunting and groaning, beat all to hell. . . . Yeah, a plenty tough one, Fraser. But still just a man who could be taken care of when the right time and chance came along. Ike Britt or one of the other boys could handle that, laying in wait along the trail with a Winchester. But the girl, that stubborn, fool girl, she was the big problem! . . .

A good hour of this sour and somber brooding went by. Over in the corner Rube Yard had quieted, whiskey-drugged into a sodden sleep. Roderick got to his feet and came around. It was high time to face the girl and lay his cards on the table. He stalked out, heavy and deliberate, pausing to squint at the bright pour of the sun. Hat pulled low, he stared at the ranch house, then headed for it.

In the office, Julie Christiansen had begun to think her estimate of Turk Roderick was at fault, that the man had curbed his impatience and was waiting for her to make the next move or advance. Increasingly uncertain and restless, she was about to desert her post when she heard the heavy scuff of boots signaling Roderick's approach. She waited for his knock tensely. None came. Instead, the office door was pushed open violently, letting him in.

The aggressive manner of his entrance and the bullying look of him brought Julie up in her chair, straight and indignant. She wasted no time in her attack, laying out her words with a crisp directness.

"You've no right in here! You are no longer any part of this ranch and never will be again. Henry Greer has instructions at the bank to pay you off. You can leave at once!"

Turk Roderick seemed not to have heard a word of it. He moved closer, squaring himself across the desk from her, his stare heavy and un-wavering. There was something almost ophidian in the dull glint of his eyes. His lips writhed under the pressure of his feelings, then went still and compressed. When he finally found words, they were harsh with a banked anger.

"You fool girl! When are you going to grow up and get some sense? When are you going to quit acting and talking like an idiot? Of course I belong on this ranch. If I wasn't here to hold things together, it wouldn't be a going ranch very long. Which your father well knew; it was the reason he left me in charge. Now while you were running away, who kept the affairs of this ranch in shape and working? I did — me — Turk Roderick! And you'd treat me like this! If Buck Christiansen was alive and here, he'd shake some sense into you!"

Julie flared hotly. "You can leave my father out of this. And I'm all through running away. This is just between you and me!"

"Right!" Roderick growled. "And I'm saying that without me to crack the whip, you'll never get a day's work out of any man on this ranch. You try to order them around, they'll laugh at you. Go ahead — try your luck!"

Speaking, he leaned forward, both hands spread on the desk. Towering above her it was as though he would impress his will upon her by sheer weight of physical bulk and a harsh, ruthless arrogance. But Julie faced him defiantly, head back and small shoulders squared.

"The men will do as I tell them or collect not a single dollar in wages. It is so arranged with Henry Greer at the bank. Nobody gets paid without written authorization from me. Go tell the men that and see who it is they laugh at. As for you, I say it again. You've no right here. Your bullying threats will do you no good. You can — get out! . . ."

Facing the harshness of his fuming stare, Julie watched slow change gather and break deep behind the brute hard glitter of his pale eyes. It was like dropping a stone into pond waters and seeing the smooth surface glint become all oily ripples. Far back an animal cunning took shape and grew. Abruptly he threw his head back and laughed. It wasn't a good laugh. . . .

"So you won't listen to reason, eh? Well, it's like you just said. Right here and now there's only you and me. And there's more than one way to make a little fool like you come to her senses. We'll see how tough you are! . . ."

He started to circle the desk and a quick terror rushed all through Julie. Her reaction was purely instinctive, and she was swiftly across the room, her back to the gun rack. Her reaching hand gripped the gun hanging there, the big Colt Peacemaker her father had taught her how to use. She hauled the gun free of its holster and pushed it level, thumbing back the spurred hammer.

"Far enough!" she warned coldly. "Don't take another step!"

Turk Roderick came to a halt, glance fixed on the round, blue snout of the gun. His eyes congested with anger and his words fell thickly.

"You wouldn't dare!"

"Try me," Julie taunted. "Go ahead — try me. Take that step!"

Instead, Roderick backed up a stride, shaking

144

his head. Here was a situation he'd never thought remotely possible and for the moment it held him bewildered and almost unbelieving. That this slip of a fool girl would dare throw down on him with a gun — on him — Turk Roderick! Here was ignominy and frustration to slug him into a sullen, wicked rage. The glare he placed on her betrayed the depth of his feelings. He could have twisted her neck, beat her with his fists, smashed her down to complete subjugation! But that big gun looking him in the eye did not waver, nor did the girl holding it. Instead, she spoke with a sort of cool detachment.

"It seems," she said, "that I am a true daughter of my father after all. I find that I have enough of his strength to do what I have to do. Which means that I will shoot if I have to. So, for the last time, get out of this house and off this ranch. And don't ever come back!"

Turk Roderick made no immediate move to obey, instead standing stiff and glowering, as though unable to come to a clear decision of any kind. Despite her brave words, Julie began to quake inside. Was this hulking brute going to leave, or wasn't he? By this time the weight of the big Colt gun was beginning to tell, and it took more and more effort to hold it level and steady.

A long moment of silence formed and grew, breathless with threat. Then, beyond the open door sounded the drum of trotting hoofs, the grate and skirl of buckboard wheels and the sharp tempo of scolding words in the unmistakable tones of an exasperated Nell Viney.

"Benny Rust. I swear there are times when you don't show a smidgin of common sense. Stop at the house, you idiot — not the corrals. You're delivering a human being, not a sack of oats! . . ."

Immediately the office tension broke. Mumbling a blurred curse, Turk Roderick wheeled to the door and out of it. On legs gone suddenly weak with relief, Julie caught at her chair to steady herself. She lowered the hammer of the gun and laid the weapon on the desk. Then she waited at the door, blinking through a mist of thankful tears.

Outside, as Nell Viney climbed down from Benny Rust's buckboard, Turk Roderick surged by, neither looking nor speaking. While brushing the dust of travel from herself, Nell Viney's wondering glance followed Roderick until he reached the bunkhouse. After which she turned and came to where Julie Christiansen waited.

Abruptly the mist of tears became a small torrent and when Nell opened her arms, Julie went into them, clinging to the older woman while gulping words of welcome. Shrewdly understanding, Nell exclaimed her concern.

"You've had trouble with that fellow Roderick?"

As Julie bobbed her head, Nell Viney's searching glance located the gun on the desk and her new words were raw with anger.

"Child, did you need that gun?"

Again Julie bobbed her head, stammering a reply.

"I — I h-had to hold him — off with it. He was — so — so crazy mad! . . . He l-looked l-like he could have killed me! . . ." Nell dredged a wisp of handkerchief from a pocket. "You poor kid! Here, use this while we talk some sense. I'm not too surprised at such a turn of events. I suspected something of the sort might take place, which is why I'm here. You can't stay on this ranch alone for another day. I'm taking you back to town with me."

Julie wiped her eyes, blew her nose and shook her head. "Nell, I can't leave. Not after facing Roderick down and saying what I did."

"What did you say?"

"I told him that I was a true daughter of my father and would do what I had to do. Even — even pull the trigger of the gun. I can't run after that."

"Nonsense!" denied Nell Viney vigorously. "You're not running away. You're merely admitting that there are some situations a lone woman can't handle by herself. Attempting to run this ranch on your own is one of such; What the ranch needs is the right man to shoulder the job — and I don't mean Turk Roderick!"

Emotions still unsettled, Julie was hesitant. "Where is there such a man? It couldn't be

147

Henry Greer. He's a banker, not a cattleman."

"There are others besides Henry Greer," Nell declared. "One, in particular. We'll talk about him later. So get what luggage you'll need and we'll be on our way."

"And leave everything unguarded, with Turk Roderick still around and running free?" Julie protested.

Nell Viney shrugged. "Child, don't rout out any unnecessary ghosts. What is this ranch? It's range and cattle. The range will always be here and the cattle are scattered over miles and miles of country. So neither Turk Roderick nor anybody else can do you any immediate harm. Now get your things together before that bumbling, but well-meaning and entirely likeable idiot, Benny Rust, forgets why he's here and drives back to town without us! . . ."

Out at Shoshone Lake a man stood beside the door of the line camp cabin and kept close watch as Orde Fraser rode in along the lakeside trail. The man was a solid chunk, short and wide, with stubby bowed legs and a barrel chest. Beneath a shaggy mop of grizzled hair, his ruddy face was round and stubborn. His shoulders were forward leaning and full of challenge. He had a Winchester across one arm and his glance was direct and searching. His spoken greeting was blunt.

"You'd better be Fraser?"

Orde Fraser's grin was brief and dry. "Happens that way. You?"

"Quider — Andy Quider. Poe Darby said you'd probably be along about now."

"And Poe — where is he?"

The rifle tipped an indicating muzzle. "Yonder somewhere. Primed for trouble and hopin' to find it."

"What kind of trouble — and why?"

Andy Quider stabbed a stubby, calloused finger at the cabin wall. "The kind that put a rifle slug right through here. Now Poe, he's out prowling, aiming to make a better shot, should he get the chance."

Fraser was quick out of his saddle. "When did this happen?"

"Right after first light this morning," Quider explained. "Poe was set to get a bucket of water from the spring. No sooner does he open the door and start to step out than the slug hits, might' near partin' Poe's hair, it's that close. Poe ducks back inside after his own gun, ready to cut down on anything that moves. But nothin' does, and when I arrive he tells me to keep an eye on things until you show up. Then he catches and saddles and goes scalp huntin'."

Orde Fraser had his look at the bullet hole. "And Poe never saw anyone?"

"So he said. By the sound of the shot he figgered it came from somewhere out toward the far end of the lake. The slug went plumb through the cabin and when I lined up the bullet holes, front and back, they pointed pretty close to that high clump of tules way out yonder. Both a man and a horse could be hid there. Makes it a pretty long shot in the early dawn half-light, which is probably why Poe is still healthy."

"Just so," Fraser agreed. "Providing the slug was really meant for Poe instead of merely a warning."

"No warning — not a chance of that," scoffed Andy Quider. "Way things been shaping up lately, ain't nobody in these parts shootin' just for the hell of it!"

Letting this flat statement ride while measuring Orde Fraser with another frank appraisal, Andy Quider went on with milder tone.

"Poe told me about you and this Shoshone Lake range. Said he had you figured as a square shooter, so was going along with you. Well, what's good enough for Poe is good enough for me. I'm ready to take the same trail."

Andy Quider's cool, blue eyes were very steady. Fraser met them with a sober statement.

"By the signs, all I can offer right now is trouble. However, once things quiet down, there'll be room on this range for all you small outfits, along with my own herd. I'm not hunting trouble and I'll go a long way to avoid it."

"No matter how far you go, it won't be enough for some," Quider said. "No trouble of course with fellers like Poe and me and Hollis Ward. Likely not with Starr Jennette, either.

Rolling C is your trouble, my friend. Buck Christiansen was a tough old pelican, but as long as you played square and stayed on your side of the trail you could live with him. When Buck got rough was when anybody tried to push him off the center of the trail. But now he's gone and it's Turk Roderick who'll be lookin' right down your throat. And Turk Roderick is all greedy, ruthless bastard! . . ."

"But Roderick is all through at Rolling C," Fraser said. "Buck Christiansen's daughter just fired him."

Andy Quider's laugh was short and mirthless. "That I got to see. Roderick won't pay her no mind. The ranch is what he wants, what he's been after for years. Now he's got it. Yeah, there's your real trouble!"

Fraser shrugged. "If so, we'll take care of it as we meet it." He turned to the packhorse. "Let's get this gear inside."

Poe Darby had been busy about the cabin. The place was swamped out, everything scrubbed. After blankets were spread on the bunks along the walls, it shaped up as a comfortable layout. While they worked, Orde Fraser covertly observed Andy Quider, measuring him, gauging his worth. What with a long, barrel body and stubby, bowed legs, the man was physically ill-proportioned. There was, however a terrier-like alertness, quick and eager. And in the steadiness of his glance burned the fires of a basic integrity. Orde

Fraser liked what he saw.

Abruptly the terrier alertness showed. Quider stiffened, head up. He reached for his rifle and wheeled to the door. "Somebody ridin' in!"

He had his look, then laughed softly. "Just Poe, back from scalp huntin'." Moving outside, he called, "Any luck?"

Poe Darby eased from his saddle. A lean old man, burned black by sun and weather, tough as a piece of rawhide whang leather. Thwarted bitterness glinted in his black eyes and his answer was gruffly brief.

"None. Picked up hoof sign but lost it in the lava brakes over south. Stir up the fire, I'm needin' my coffee." He stacked his rifle and turned to Orde Fraser. "Andy tell you?"

Fraser nodded. "Dry-gulch lead is mean stuff, Poe — too mean for you and Andy to risk on my account."

Poe growled his sharp impatience. "Quit that talk. When I draw cards in a game, I play the hand out. Same goes for Andy."

At the stove and listening, Andy Quider added his quick assent. "Just so! And still no idea, Poe?"

"No more than a guess. Most likely somebody from Rolling C."

"Like Ike Britt — or Rube Yard?"

"Not Yard." Poe paused to lay a glance of warm approval on Orde Fraser. "While ridin' I met up with Hollis Ward and one of his men pushing a little gather of Ward's stuff toward the home range. Hollis told me what happened in town last night. Said he never saw a man take a more complete curryin' than the one Fraser here handed out to Rube Yard."

Andy Quider came quickly around. "Hey — hey! What's this — what's this?" He looked at Fraser. "Tell me? . . ."

Orde Fraser's smile was small, his answer quiet. "Had a little misunderstanding with Yard, is all."

"Misunderstanding — hell!" snorted Poe, waving a scoffing hand. "Hollis said that when you finished with Rude Yard he looked half dead."

Andy Quider swore soulfully. "Be damned! Never fails. I was set to hit town last night, but changed my mind. Thereby missin' all the fun."

Again Fraser showed his small, quiet smile, while laying a finger on his jaw where Nell Viney had touched. "Wasn't all fun, Andy. Now let's get some grub on the table before Poe folds up."

He made do with a cup of coffee while Poe and Andy ate hungrily. Done with food, Poe's glance lifted. "You're callin' the turns. What now?"

"A ride," Fraser said. "You and me. I want to get some idea of the limits of my range. Andy, you stick close here — and don't make a target of yourself."

They circled the lake at a jog. The sun, well up by this time, laid its warm flare across the water, where ripples ran and sparkled before a vagrant breeze. Small wildlife teemed, the tules alive with marsh sparrows. Long skeins of blackbirds rose, swooped away, then wheeled back. Killdeer fled along marshy shores, their startled crying a plaintive, wistful note under the wide sky and big country all round about. Well out from shore the mallard pair of yesterday rested while, closer in, a solitary helldriver threaded its quick, predatory way, reptilian head and neck cocked and alert for some luckless minnow.

Water — water! Other names for it, Orde Fraser mused, might well be gold, and life. For where it existed and endured, there too did life!

Once clear of the lake, Poe Darby began dropping laconic remarks across his shoulder. "No fences in this country, so range limits are mostly just geography and a general idea. Few natural boundaries outside the rim and an occasional dry wash goin' nowhere. Out this way your range and Rolling C meet shoulder to shoulder in spots. Buck Christiansen always figgered Hayfork Crossing as his eastern limit, so we might as well head out there."

With the fires of his early morning anger still simmering, Poe Darby rode high in his saddle, his head swinging constantly, his glance raking and probing the different distances, close in and far out. Wire-lean and alert, he made Orde Fraser think of a vengeful old wolf.

The country ran away in long, rolling sweeps;

here a slight rise, there a sprawling flat. Scattered through the clumps of sage, range grass sprouted, turned rich and brown by sun and season. On all sides, cattle were searching out this fodder.

Here, too, when they passed close enough, Fraser read brands and, as it had been around Shoshone Lake, the Rolling C iron was in greatest evidence. One small hollow held a full dozen head and after looking them over, Poe Darby twisted in his saddle.

"You see? All Rolling C stuff. And that outfit ain't about to let go of any of this grass unless forced to."

"In which case," said Orde Fraser dryly, "they'll be forced!"

"And that," pointed out Poe sententiously, "will mean fight!"

"Quite probably," Fraser agreed. "But if that's the way it must be — then that is the way it will be."

CHAPTER IX

It was close to midday when they rode in at Hayfork Crossing. A meager collection of sun-dried, weatherbeaten shacks sprawled along a single dusty street that at one time had been part of a stage and freight road that came winding through the sage from the west and now lost itself in more of the same kind of country to the east.

The largest building centered the place. A warped hitch rail sagged tiredly in front of the building. At it now were two saddle mounts drowsily switching flies. Poe Darby hauled up beside them and made blunt observation.

"Swede Soderman's layout. Nothing to look at, but the whiskey and the food are as good as you'll find anywhere, and right now I could stand some of both, it being that time of day. How about it?"

Orde Fraser's answer was to swing down, tie, and follow Poe into a barroom that was hot and dingy. In a shadowed corner the owners of the saddle ponies outside were intent at some card game. They gave brief survey to Fraser and Poe then turned back to their game.

Behind the bar, Swede Soderman waited. He was a bony, wrinkled man with an untidy mop of tow hair, and his faded eyes seemed to reflect a sad fatalism. Still simmering somewhat from his morning misadventure, Poe reacted curtly.

"What's gravelin' you this time, Swede? That God-hates-me look you're packin' could break a strong man's heart. Mister Fraser here, and me, we're wantin' a drink or two and then a bait of grub. If supplyin' those things are too much for you to handle, say so plain out and we'll move along."

Swede lifted a placating hand. "Ain't fellers like you, Poe. It's other people."

So saying, Swede swung a quick and cautious glance at the two card players. He set out bottle and glasses while making further careful and lugubrious complaint.

"What's gravelin' me, you ask? All right, I'll tell you. Time was when a man could figger pretty close to what tomorrow would bring. But no more — not around here, anyway. This part of the world is due to come apart."

Poe poured the drinks, then eyed Swede severely past a half-lifted glass. "You sure don't spread any sunshine. If you're drivin' at something, say it plain."

Swede shrugged narrow, bony shoulders. "When Buck Christiansen was alive, a man could know where he stood. Old Buck was tough, but he was solid and he sort of anchored the world for a lot of us folks. But Buck's gone now and a wild man is runnin' his spread. Even worse than that, from talk I hear, Long Les Blackwell is pointed this way. And he's poison!"

Up to this point Orde Fraser had been mildly amused at the trading of words. But now he came up intent and frowning.

"A minute, friend! What's this about Les Blackwell — and why is he poison, as you call it?"

Hesitant at first, Swede Soderman now showed a flare of spirit. "A feller like me, pourin' likker across a bar, he hears a lot that other folks miss. Stray cowpokes drift in, thirsty and lonely. A couple of drinks loosens them up and they begin to talk. I listen. Sometimes I listen damn close, and so I hear things. Now I'll tell you about Long Les Blackwell. He's poison because when he moves in on a stretch of range, it generally ends up with him shovin' everybody else off it. And when he's got ideas that way, he always sends in Fitch Carlin to get the dirty job done. Right now I hear that Fitch Carlin is already on his way, bringin' in a herd off Blackwell's Owyhee range. And Fitch Carlin, he's worse than poison! Now, what will it be for grub?"

Before Fraser could speak, Poe cut in. "Steak, spuds and coffee. And mebbe a piece of pie?"

Swede Soderman headed for the door of a back room. "I'll go get Sophie started."

Pouring a second drink, Poe Darby faced Orde Fraser with a gruff apology. "Wasn't

158

meanin' to shut you off. But Swede, once he gets started at complainin' about this and that, he's like to go on forever. I just headed him off before we starved to death."

For a thoughtful moment or two, Fraser did not answer while pushing his glass around and around on the bar top. Then he shrugged.

"Doesn't matter."

Only — it did matter!

This was the second time he'd heard Les Blackwell and Fitch Carlin spoken of in such a manner and in similar terms. First time was from Starr Jennette, and now from Swede Soderman. Also, where Long Les Blackwell was concerned, there was the reserved and sober manner in which banker Henry Greer had accepted L. J. Blackwell's draft.

No doubt Starr Jennette's word had come from the same source as had Swede Soderman's. And, mused Fraser, as he had reasoned before, if there was a herd coming in from the Owyhee, it could very well be the one Blackwell had promised him back when they had met at Winnemucca. However, there was that hint of wariness on the part of both Soderman and Jennette, which couldn't be discarded with a shrug. And though Swede was plainly a mild, timid soul — the sort to see a ghost behind every sage thicket — Starr Jennette was made of far sterner stuff.

Too, what about this fellow, Fitch Carlin? Someone Orde Fraser had never met, knowing

159

of him only through hearsay. But there still remained the way the man was spoken of — always as though he rode in a big saddle, a very big and ruthless saddle! Fraser was still pondering the whole proposition over a half-empty glass when Swede Soderman returned.

"Sophie says you're to come out back!"

In the strongest kind of contrast to her husband and his somewhat sleazy barroom, Sophia Soderman and her kitchen were pin neat and orderly. She was a prim, bird-like little soul, with a snapping spirit in her glance as she looked Orde Fraser over carefully before turning to Poe Darby with words as sharp as her glance.

"Poe Darby, you certainly don't improve any with age. You're near to being an affront to the human race. Last time you sat at my table must have been near a year ago, and now you're just as mangy as ever. When was the last time you bought a new shirt?"

Poe's grin stretched his leathery cheeks. "Just like an old sun-cured boot, that's me, Sophie. Not quite useless yet, but movin' close. So what would I want with a new shirt? This'n I got on ain't near wore through yet."

Sophie sniffed her disdain. "Maybe not worn through, but scruffy as a half-starved coyote. Now, long as you're here to eat, sit up — sit up!"

The food was plain, plentiful and good; topped off with a generous wedge of dried

160

apple pie. Over this, Poe smacked his lips.

"Sophie," said he, "should Swede ever get mad enough to run you out of the house, you come look for me. I'll find you a new home."

Listening in at the doorway, Swede Soderman cackled thinly. "Anybody gets run out of the house, it'll be me, not Sophie."

The meal done, Orde Fraser laid a couple of dollars on the table and saluted Sophia Soderman with approving words.

"The kind of food, ma'am, to bring a man back to this table real often. Remembering it will make it easier to ride this way again."

The bird-like little woman beamed. "You hear that, Soderman? And you, Poe Darby? That was a gentleman speaking, giving you a lesson in manners."

Poe grinned again. "I'll remember, Sophie — and try my luck next time."

Swede Soderman followed them out to the hitch rail and stood staring off to the east. From his saddle, Poe called down.

"You mebbe see somethin' out there, Swede?"

Soderman shook his head. "Not yet, I don't. But I'm expectin' to most any time. Like a drift of dust tellin' of a herd comin' in from the Owyhee. I got a feelin' about that herd, and I'm tellin' the world it ain't a good feelin'! . . . ."

Poe reined quickly away, drawing Fraser with him. "Got to get out of here before Swede gives me the dismals, too."

Save for a wider swing to the south, they

went back much the way they came. Most of the ride was made in silence, Poe Darby being a taciturn man by nature and Orde Fraser caught up with thought, musing on Swede Soderman's mood and final comments. With impatience spurring him, Fraser was glad to haul up at Shoshone Lake. Not immediately in evidence, Andy Quider showed presently, coming in from behind the lava outcrop, leading both his own horse and the pack animal Fraser had brought out from town.

"Aimed to get everything out of sight," Andy explained. "So if anybody figgered the place empty and came snoopin', I'd have them dead to rights."

"Using your head," Fraser approved. "Now I'm for town. Mail could be in tonight and I'm expecting some that will explain several things to me."

"Just so," Poe Darby growled. "Meanwhile, you'll be watchin' the trail ahead and behind as well as on both sides. Because it's shapin' up as that kind of a world now for people like us! . . ."

Wasting no time along the town trail, Orde Fraser pushed the dun to a pace that kept the packhorse at a shuffling trot behind. A soberness of thought rode with Fraser, together with a vague but persistent unease. It was this unease that puzzled and irritated him, because he could not figure any good reason for it. Puzzled him because after all there were the facts as he knew them. First of all, there was his inheritance: solidly real and permanent. Next, from banker L. J. Blackwell — or Long Les Blackwell if the natives insisted on it that way — had come substantial financial support, together with the promise of further backing in the way of enough breeder stock to furnish the beginnings of a herd for his Shoshone Lake range. And where would such cattle come from if not from Blackwell's Owyhee holdings, the closest and most accessible?

Such were the facts as he knew them. All else, like Swede Soderman's nasal vaporings, was just conjecture based on rumor or what Starr Jennette had called whiskey talk. . . .

So much for logical and realistic conclusions, Fraser reasoned. Still and all, as he rode, there persisted that edge of unease that he could not shake. . . .

From the warm gloom of the Rolling C bunkhouse, Turk Roderick watched Julie Christiansen and Nell Viney carry a few items of luggage out to Benny Rust's buckboard, climb to the seat beside him and roll away town-ward. Sullen and foul of mood, Roderick knew he had overplayed matters badly in threatening to lay rough hands on the girl who defied and scorned him so scathingly. Now — what to do — what to do? . . .

With the buckboard fast disappearing in a swirl of amber dust, Roderick once again crossed to the ranch office where he threw himself into the desk chair and slouched down, scowling and brooding, seeking to arrive at some line of action he might benefit by. Facing him were two choices. Either he pack his warbag and head for new and distant parts, letting go of all dreams of owning any part of Rolling C; or he stay on in this Humboldt Rim country, make the big gamble and, however ruthless and savage it had to be, fight to make the gamble good.

The gamble would be the taking over of the Shoshone Lake range with the line cabin as a base and carrying on from there. In part, it was something he'd already been working at, intending to add that stretch to the other Rolling C holdings. In this his methods had been brutal and direct, moving everybody else off by whatever means necessary. He had burned out Shep Riley and Poe Darby and Andy Quider, and when Riley refused to take the hint and moved into the Shoshone Lake cabin, he'd had Riley dragged to death down the main street of Humboldt City as a warning to all else who would oppose him.

Right now he had Ike Britt, the rider who had dragged Riley, out prowling the Shoshone Lake country, hoping for a chance to dry-gulch Darby or Quider or Starr Jennette; the latter being not only someone whom he hated virulently, but also feared. Hollis Ward didn't count anymore, being old and weak and wanting only peace. A mere harsh warning would take care of Hollis Ward. True, a new and unexpected obstacle had shown up to clutter the trail — that fellow Fraser. Tough one there, but still only one man, and mortal. Some careful planning could take care of him! . . .

The more he considered it, the better the picture looked. Any question of right or law did not enter. Maybe Dan Larkin did pack some authority inside the limits of Humboldt City, but anywhere out on the open range it would be mere possession that counted. And when he, Turk Roderick, possessed Shoshone Lake, who was to move him off?

Spurred on by the arrogance and conceit that was so much a part of his makeup, the decision solidified. When it did, he felt immediately better, shedding the mood of baffled frustration that had begun to dog him. And as for that fool girl with her silly ideas, there were any number of ways he could get even with her. Rolling C was a big, rich outfit, ripe to be raided. Right now the Shoshone Lake range was crowded with Rolling C cattle, and with him dug in on that range, the cattle would stay there!

No living person but himself knew better the exact limits of Rolling C range, or the number of cattle carrying that brand, or the real meat of its affairs as did he. Buckley Christiansen had known these things, for he had fashioned and built them. But Buckley Christiansen now was dead. And only a man who knew how these things had been put together, better knew how to take them apart. That man was himself! So reasoned Turk Roderick.

The thought brought him to his feet. Rising on his toes he reared to his full height. In him the move was sinister, one of dark and ruthless purpose. One part of the beginning was in the bunkhouse and the time to start was now! . . .

The bunkhouse water bucket stood on a bench just inside the door. On a nail above it hung a tin dipper. Scooping the dipper full of water, Turk Roderick stepped over to the blanket-tumbled bunk on which Rube Yard sprawled in unlovely sleep. With measured deliberation Roderick sloshed the contents of the dipper into Rube's battered, bruise-stained face. Reaction was a muffled groan, a mumbled curse and a hand waved limply as though to brush aside some minor annoyance. After which, Rube slipped back into the depths.

A second time, Roderick emptied a dipper of water over Rube's face and head. But it took a third and fourth application of the treatment to bring Rube shakily back to a world of cruel reality. He pushed up on one elbow, full of misery and mumbled profanity.

At the far end of the bunkhouse, a door led to the cook shack. Through that door Roderick called curt order. "Put on a pot of coffee, Smokie. Make it strong. Bring it and your whiskey bottle in here."

About to turn back, Roderick cocked his head, listening. Outside, a horse had come to a weary halt. Ike Britt swung from the saddle and shuffled heavily through the bunkhouse door where Turk Roderick met him with blunt greeting.

"Time you showed up. What you been doing?"

"Trying to move in on the Shoshone Lake line camp. What you wanted, wasn't it?"

"Not just trying," Roderick returned with some harshness. "We need more than that."

Ike Britt's shrug was sullen. "Somebody already there."

"Somebody there! Who?"

"Poe Darby for one. Andy Quider for another."

"You mean they're living in the line cabin?"

Ike Britt shrugged again. "That's it." He was a surly, foul, slug of a man.

"A pair of old fossils," scoffed Roderick. "And you let them scare you off? Had your gun, didn't you?"

"Sure I had my gun, same as always. Wasn't scared, either. Just a little careful. Because that pair of old fossils can be tough as hell when the chips are down. You don't waltz right up and spit in the eye of either one of them unless you're tired of livin' — which I ain't. I did make a try for Darby, but the setup wasn't right. The morning light was too poor and the range too far. So I missed."

While speaking, Ike Britt stared past Roderick at Rube Yard's sprawled figure in its pit of misery. "What happened to him?"

"Made a damn fool of himself and ran into something."

Ike Britt's meager grin was just a slight twitch of his heavy lips. "Must have been with a freight train." Then, as he added more, his tone became heavy with dark surliness. "Don't you rawhide me, Turk. I been doin' the best I could. But nobody can shoot center every try. Also, I been siwashin' it out in the lava roughs, sleepin' damn hard and cold and eatin' light. When I've fed and had a good sleep, I'll give it another try. But meanwhile, don't you try rawhidin' me! . . ."

Turk Roderick did not argue the point. Handled right, Ike Britt was a valuable part of his planning for the future. Because Ike Britt was the sort to take orders and follow them blindly; no matter how foul or deadly savage they were, or where they led. It was like Ike Britt who dragged Shep Riley to death and he was a prime one to lay in wait along some trail and shoot an unwary man in the back. At the same time, like any other dull, slinking brute, he could turn savagely dangerous if aroused to it by too heavy a hand of authority.

Thoroughly aware of this, Turk Roderick now spoke mildly. "Sure, Ike — sure. Wasn't meaning to rawhide you. Soon as Smokie gets done with what I want, he'll cook up a good feed for you. Then you can catch up on your sleep and make another try later. And, Ike, never pass up a chance at Starr Jennette or that new feller, Fraser, who claims he owns the Shoshone Lake layout. For we need that place in our business."

"Hell!" grunted Britt. "I already had that figgered."

"Thought you might," Roderick approved. He nodded toward Rube Yard. "Now I got to get him up and riding and useful again."

Smokie Gant came in from the cook shack, laden with what Roderick had called for. Lank, long-faced and droop-shouldered, Smokie Gant was one content to say little, follow orders, and live out his days in the sanctuary of his kitchen world. The whiskey bottle he brought was half full. From this Roderick poured a heavy jolt into a cup and topped it off with black coffee. He caught Rube Yard by a shoulder, hauled him up to a sitting position and held the cup to his battered lips.

"Get outside it," he ordered harshly. "Put it down. There's more to come!"

Grunting and gulping, Rube obeyed. Followed a second cup that held straight coffee, as did a third and part of a fourth. Unable to manage another swallow, Rube slouched forward, head hanging, stolid and unresponsive. Turk Roderick quickened matters with another dipper of water, a deluge that brought blurted protest from Rube.

"A'right — a'right, lay off that damned water. I'm comin' out of the fog. What you want of me, anyhow?"

Roderick did not answer, instead turning to Smokie Gant. "Cook up a good feed for Ike and let him have the rest of the bottle if he wants it."

Ike Britt was swift with his reach for the bottle. "He wants it!" And he carried it with him as he followed Smokie Gant back into the cook shack.

Wiping a careful hand across his face, Rube Yard hiccoughed heavily and repeated his fretful query. "What you want with me? I ain't in no shape to sit a saddle and chouse cattle."

"You're not about to chouse cows," Roderick told him. "At least, not for a while. Right now something more important is ahead for you. Come night you'll feel better about sitting a saddle, plenty good enough to be on your way back to town to even up with that fellow, Fraser, the one who worked you over. Yeah, you'll locate him and even up — good!"

Rube considered these words in dull, morose silence. Never overly alert mentally, just now his thoughts were particularly heavy and sluggish and, awakening them enough to get the full limits of what Roderick was suggesting, became a slow and painful task. Some little time passed before it began to register, to shake clear of the mixed-up tangle in his mind. When it did finally quicken, it lighted a spark that brought him up a little straighter, focusing his blurred glance into reasonable steadiness and producing a mumbled protest.

"No way I can settle accounts with him — not with these." He lifted both fists. "He already proved that to me."

"Who said anything about fists?" Roderick retorted. "You can still handle a gun, can't you?"

Rube's shoulders sagged again. "Ain't got a gun. Fraser — he took my gun away from me."

"Plenty of guns around," Roderick said quickly. "I'll get you one. But first I want to know — are you interested?"

Rube brooded over this until the spark took hold again and brightened steadily. His head came up. "How you mean?"

Turk Roderick took a short turn up and down the bunkhouse. "Like this," he said. "You ride in tonight and leave your horse on the flats outside of town. It will be plenty dark along the street under the cottonwoods. A man standing still and quiet under those trees in the dark could be there all night without anybody knowing he was there. Now Fraser is almost certain to be in town and will be moving around some. Pretty soon he could come by you real close and you could make dead sure of him. He'd never know what hit him! And before anybody can figure what's happened, you'll be back to your horse and gone, with nobody able to prove a single thing except that Fraser is damn good and dead!"

There was a persuasive confidence in the picture Turk Roderick drew and, liking what he saw, the beckoning spark in Rube was brightened to a living flame. He lunged to unsteady feet.

"Get me that gun! . . ."

"Right away," Roderick promised. "Meanwhile, clean yourself up and take on some food. Keep moving around. Come night you'll be as good as ever."

Picking a careful way, Rube headed back into the cook shack while Turk Roderick crossed again to the ranch office. The gun Julie Christiansen had used to face him down — old Buck Christiansen's gun — still lay on the desk. Roderick picked up the big Peacemaker and balanced it on his palm. He liked the irony behind its next deadly usage, and a corner of his mouth lifted in a sardonic grimace as he considered Ike Britt and Rube Yard.

Two of a kind, that pair. Dull, unimaginative, far down on the human scale, but perfect tools for what he had in mind. With both of them on the prowl seeking a chance at Orde Fraser, one or the other of them must surely get the job done. Each of them, in his own way, knew a perverted brute-savage pride in the sort of foul business he had set them on. So a smart man could use them and profit thereby. . . .

And should it come about that they blundered along their savage way and ended up dead before the gun of a better man, who cared — who would ever care? . . . Again, hefting the gun in his hand, Turk Roderick went back to the bunkhouse.

CHAPTER X

Afternoon was slipping away across the rim when Orde Fraser hauled to a stop at Benny Rust's livery barn. Standing in the first reach of sundown shadow, Benny eyed the dun with professional interest.

"You sure bought that horse to use, didn't you?"

"That's right," Fraser said, swinging down. "He gets special feeding again tonight. Something extra for the pack bronc, too."

Benny took over the dun's rein. "Very first thing, you're to report at the hotel. Miss Nell said so."

About to turn away, Fraser paused. "Something real important?"

Benny shrugged. "Depends, I guess. All I know is what she told me to tell you. Past that I'm to keep my mouth shut. Which I aim to do. You want more, ask her."

Fraser nodded and went on up the street, searching the area in front of Wash Butterfield's store for some sign of the Iron Mountain stage, but finding none. Knowing a gust of disappointment, he cut over to the hotel, his glance probing the belt of smoke-blue shadow shrouding the rim's dark face. Above that swimming

173

sea of soft, luring color, the crest of the rim was all aflame with sunset fire.

Though but a few short days under its great, frowning presence, Fraser had already begun to regard the massive black scarp with something akin to reverence. It was, he thought, bound to affect any mere mortal that way.

Nell Viney was behind the register desk. She inclined her red head toward the hotel parlor.

"In there. And," she added tartly, "mind your manners and don't act the usual stiff-necked male critter. Somebody in there needs a strong shoulder to lean on and I've decided you own that shoulder."

Fraser stared. "Woman, you talk in riddles. What the devil are you driving at?"

Again, Nell Viney indicated the parlor. "Go find out. And don't forget to be human!"

Thoroughly baffled, Fraser stepped into the hotel parlor. As she had been when he first visited with her in this room, Julie Christiansen sat on the old sofa, elbow on knee, chin couched in her hand. Now she came quickly to her feet with a show of hesitant eagerness.

"This is very kind of you, Mr. Fraser. I know I have little right to any part of your time or attention, but I'm hoping that what I have to say will interest you."

Startled at facing a new and different image, Orde Fraser stood quietly, trying to bring this image into clear focus and to understand the reason for it. From the very first moment he glimpsed her, this girl had persisted in claiming a place in his mind. At that time he had thought to consider her in a strictly impersonal, objective way: seeing her of course as very attractive, with a young and appealing air of uncertainty toward life and its problems. But now he had found that impersonal judgement was not enough. She was much more than just a breath of elusive fragrance, or a shade of warm color briefly glimpsed and swiftly gone. Studying her now, he saw grace and beauty; and the awareness he had known when she stood robe-wrapped beside him in his room, looking down at a street where a hapless little brush popper had just been dragged to death, returned now stronger than ever.

He spoke quietly. "I'll be glad to listen."

She had not missed the depth of his intent regard, or the show of quickening feeling behind it. Color washed her cheeks and her hesitancy increased. Then her slim shoulders squared and her chin lifted.

"What I wanted to see you about was to offer you a job."

Again, Fraser was startled into a moment of pause. Then he shook his head. "I'm in no position to hire out, Miss Christiansen. My own affairs will take all my time. Of course I appreciate your offer."

Disappointment clouded her eyes and the hesitancy returned. "I was afraid your first reaction would be that way. But I am hoping that when I explain more fully, you'll reconsider."

"What is that job?" Fraser asked.

"That you become foreman of my ranch, the Rolling C. I have discharged the man who held that job and I need someone who is capable of taking over in his place." She said it almost defiantly, as though the embers of her stormy showdown with Turk Roderick still glowed.

Again Orde Fraser shook his head. "I truly wish I could help you, but I can't. It just wouldn't work out, as I couldn't handle your ranch properly while taking care of my own." He considered a moment before adding, "I can suggest a good man in my place. Starr Jennette."

"No!" The reply was quick and definite. "That would never do. It would not be fair to him." She moved to the door. "I'm sorry. I guess I had no right to expect anything different. And I must quit running to you with my troubles! . . ."

After which she was quickly gone, across the foyer and up the stairs.

Alone, Orde Fraser stood held in moody thought and, for some obscure reason, he was thoroughly dissatisfied with himself. He certainly owed nothing to Julie Christiansen, yet the sense of having failed her caught and held him as he went to his room, there to wash up. Later, when the supper call jangled and he came down, Nell Viney faced him in the dining room and eyed him accusingly.

"I've half a mind to turn you out minus your supper. Because you let her down and you let me down. You didn't offer the shoulder I asked for."

"What else could I do?" Fraser defended. "I've a ranch of my own to put on a working basis, and from all the signs so far, that will keep me plenty busy."

Nell Viney turned abruptly away, but later came by his table to drop a light hand on his shoulder. "Forgive a nosy old woman! I've no right to turn scratchy. It's just that I think so much of that girl. For though she's a young woman grown, and a lovely one — as you may have noticed — in some ways she's still a babe in the woods. All the fault being that of her father, a well-meaning but in some ways a bumbling old pirate, Buckley Christiansen."

"I helped her all I could," Fraser said. "I gave her the name of a good man in my place, but she said no to that."

"What man?"

"Starr Jennette."

Nell Viney tossed her hands in mock despair. "You men! You thick-headed, impossible male critters! Of all others, you had to mention him!"

"Well, why not? What's wrong with Starr?" Fraser defended. "I see him as a damn good man, one nobody can push around. In particular, Turk Roderick and his bucko crowd."

"That," Nell Viney agreed, "might very well

be. But as riding boss of Julie Christiansen's ranch, it wouldn't do — it wouldn't ever do!"

"You women folks can sure talk in riddles," Fraser accused. "When I named him, Miss Christiansen said 'no,' real quick, that it wouldn't be fair to him. I can't figure that."

"Very simple," Nell Viney said. "Starr Jennette was Buckley Christiansen's choice, but he wasn't Julie's and never could be. Also, no honest person ever encourages an impossible relationship. And Julie Christiansen is thoroughly honest. There's your answer."

She went away then and presently it was Town Marshal Dan Larkin who slid into the chair across from Fraser, bringing with him his usual deep-toned gruffness.

"Glad to see you still healthy."

"Any good reason why I shouldn't be?" Fraser returned.

Larkin jerked a shoulder. "Some pretty murky things in the works. Anything can happen."

"Such as? . . ." encouraged Fraser. Then, when Larkin did not answer immediately, he added, "Or are you going mysterious on me, too? When I rode in this evening, Benny Rust was solemn as a billy owl. Acted like he had something on his mind so heavy it was weighing him plumb down into his socks. And now Nell Viney just finished giving me a little assortment of left-handed hell. What the devil's wrong? What's it all about, anyhow?"

178

"Like this," Larkin rumbled. "Yesterday, Julie Christiansen went out to take over at Rolling C. Today Nell Viney rode out with Benny Rust and brought her back. I knew something was wrong, but when I tried to get something from Nell, she wouldn't talk. So then I tackled Benny. Like you say, he was so full of news he was ready to bust, but he tried to stall me, too. I put some weight on him and finally he gave it to me. Julie Christiansen had to throw a gun on Turk Roderick to keep him civilized!"

Orde Fraser stiffened, his glance boring at Larkin. "The hell! That fellow Roderick is asking for a shroud!"

Larkin nodded. "My own thought. Now you know."

One of the Indian girls brought Larkin his supper and he dug in hungrily. Caught up in thought, Fraser ate more leisurely. He now had the problem between Julie Christiansen and Starr Jennette well figured. Understanding why she wouldn't consider Jennette as riding boss and why it wouldn't be fair to the man. Because Jennette might hope again when there was no hope.

What Larkin had just told him had stirred up a quickening impatience at the way his thoughts were moving. Of what real concern for him were these old and deep-seated troubles of other people? Why, frankly, should he give a damn? Why should he care? In an attempt to put it all aside, he made blunt query of the marshal.

"The stage isn't in yet. It often run this late?"

"Once in a while." Larkin paused between bites. "Long drag from Iron Mountain and things can happen. The stage is an old one and I've often wondered how it's held together this long. Then again, harness can break or one of the team pick up a stone bruise and go lame. But if it's the mail that's worrying you — don't! The mail sack will get here if Bill Weeks has to haul it in on his back."

Finished with his meal, Larkin packed his pipe and headed out, trailing tobacco smoke. Fraser left a little later, going up to his room after his gun. He'd left the weapon there while he ate, but now, bound for the street, he buckled it on, recalling the warning Poe Darby had rendered out at Shoshone Lake.

"It's that kind of world for us, now! . . ."

On the edge of the hotel porch he paused to smoke out the last of his after-supper cigarette. The night was thick dark, the rim a great black bulwark shouldering into a velvet sky that had begun to show the first scattering of stars. A small, keen wind sifted along the street, bringing with it a creaking of wheel spokes and the shuffling tempo past to haul up at Butterfield's.

Caught up with a new eagerness, Orde Fraser spun his cigarette butt into the street's dust and left the porch. Maybe he'd learn now just what was what and where he stood. . . .

The usual gather of curious ones had drifted in at Butterfield's store where Bill Weeks was explaining the reason for his delay.

"Train from Winnemucca was late. And I wasn't about to leave without the mail. Ain't any hell of a lot of it, anyhow."

Wash Butterfield emptied the mail sack on his counter and skimmed through the contents quickly. When finished he looked up, caught Orde Fraser's eye, and shook his head.

"Nothing here for you."

"You sure? . . ."

Butterfield upended the sack and shook it a second time. "See for yourself." Glimpsing the sharp shade of disappointment on Fraser's face, the storekeeper added, "Sorry! . . ."

About to turn away to the door, Fraser nodded. "Not your fault, of course. Maybe better luck next trip."

Out on the store porch, Fraser stood with his brooding thoughts. Next trip — next trip, when? At its best two long days away, day after tomorrow. Hell with that! For today was today and tomorrow was tomorrow. And in the meantime he was pawing the ground to get started. And to get a feeling of certainty about certain things, too. . . .

Those who had gathered at the store began drifting away into the night. Counting the long evening ahead, Fraser thought of his room with distaste, being far too restless to cage up so

181

early. Up and across the street, the lights of Pete Eagle's Ten High Bar offered welcome, so he headed there. A few customers were lined against the bar, while four others were taking chairs around a poker table, one of them breaking open a fresh deck of cards. Fraser moved up to the table, dropping a quiet question.

"Room for a fifth, maybe?"

They looked him over, then gave assenting nods. One of them spoke, "Five-handed always makes for a better game of stud."

Fraser drew up a chair and bought a stack of chips. He played automatically and with indifferent success, because his mind was elsewhere. After an hour of this he knew it was no cure for the restlessness that was dogging him; so he bought a round of drinks, cashed in and left, not sure of a destination until he glimpsed the yellow eye of a light in Dan Larkin's office.

The breeze coming down off the rim and running along the street had quickened. A wide wash of stars glittered coldly in the sky, but their light was not enough to cut through the inky gloom under the cottonwoods. And now, as Orde Fraser moved through this deep dark, out of nowhere and quite abruptly, a thread of prescience rippled up his spine. For on the wind pushing at his cheeks rode the strong odor of cigarette smoke. At the same moment and close ahead sounded a faint stir of stealthy movement.

Prescience became a screaming clarion of warning. Drawing his gun as he moved, Orde Fraser whirled aside, bumping into and then slightly behind a trunk of a cottonwood. Out in front and close at hand a gun blared its heavy report, the flame of it a lashing, blue-crimson rip in the inky dark. To Fraser it seemed he almost felt the impact of the heavy, seeking slug smashing into the tree trunk that partially sheltered him. Bullet-torn bark fragments struck and stung his face.

Came a second rumble of report and burst of gun flame and scatter of bullet-ripped bark. Following this there was a lunging rush of movement as the gunman began to run. Making his guess at the second spike of gunflame, Fraser threw a shot, then followed with another quick try, shifting the lay of his gun ever so slightly. This time, against the authority of the gun's heavy voice, he heard the soggy strike of hurtling lead. Right after, there sounded the slithering fall of a body and a guttering, fading sigh.

Came a long moment of dead silence, as though a startled world was holding its breath. But quickly came the roll of men's voices and the thud of their running feet. A questioning shout lifted.

"Over here," Fraser answered. "And bring a light." Marshal Dan Larkin arrived along with a man carrying a lantern, the marshal's harsh growl heavy with authority. "What goes — what goes?"

Fraser kept his reply fairly even. "Whoever it was is down out there ahead, Dan. This is Fraser."

"And that doesn't surprise me too much," Larkin rumbled. "Bring that damn lantern closer."

The meager glow of the lantern disclosed a figure face down in the street's dust. Dan Larkin had his look, then exclaimed his findings.

"Rube Yard! Which doesn't surprise me, either, as he's long been slated for this kind of finish. All right, friend Fraser — tell it!"

"I'd just left a poker game in the Ten High and was headed for your office. Of a sudden, close ahead of me, there was cigarette smoke — strong! That warned me and I ducked for cover behind a cottonwood. Didn't get all the way there, but far enough, luckily. He tried for me twice and chewed bark off that sheltering tree. Then — I got him. It was the cigarette smoke that saved my skin."

"It all adds up," Larkin said. "Go along to my office and wait for me there. Rest of you men give me a hand."

When Dan Larkin came into his office some quarter of an hour later, Orde Fraser was seated quietly there, his jaw line tight-drawn, his glance brooding and straight ahead. Larkin tossed a gun on his desk.

"That's what he made his try with. And I know the gun. Buck Christiansen carried it for years. Son, you were lucky!"

"Yes and no," Fraser said tersely. "You kill a man, you kill some part of yourself."

"Depends on the why of it," Larkin said. "When a man's hand is forced, what else can he do? Justification levels everything, I know, because I've been there a couple of times." He tapped the gun before him. "This had me wondering. Did Rube figure it all out by himself or did somebody else figure it for him? How else would he have got hold of Buck Christiansen's gun?"

Restless, Orde Fraser got up to move about the room, pausing finally at the open door, staring out into the night. Presently, he turned back to face Dan Larkin across the desk.

"I don't know about the gun, but I do know this. Earlier tonight Julie Christiansen asked me to take on as riding boss of Rolling C. I turned her down then, but now I've changed my mind. It's something I've got to do, Dan — take over out there. It's the only way I can get that outfit off my back. This affair with Rube Yard just proves it. If I don't cool them off, the kind of luck I had tonight won't last forever. Sooner or later, one of them will get me. I go out there, I'll take that gun with me and jam it down somebody's throat if I have to. I'll go find out if the job offer is still open. It is, I'll be back for the gun."

He crossed quickly to the hotel, where a tense silence held. The only person in sight was one of the Indian girls, wielding a broom in the

185

dining room. She faced Fraser, wide-eyed with a wary excitement. The word, Fraser realized, had reached here.

"Miss Nell?" he queried.

The Indian girl pointed at the kitchen door. Fraser knocked, opened the door and stepped through. Both Nell Viney and Julie Christiansen were there and he clearly read the question in their regard.

"It was Rube Yard and forced on me," he told them simply. "I had no choice. A rough few minutes, but over with. I can live with it if you can, Miss Christiansen. You offered me a job this afternoon and I refused. I have come now to ask for that job. Riding boss of Rolling C. I want to take over and clean things up out there. That is — if you still want me."

"The answer, of course, is yes!" put in Nell Viney quickly.

The girl lifted a hesitant hand. "Even after what happened tonight — you still feel you can manage such men? There's bound to be more like Rube Yard, Mr. Fraser."

"Had I thought otherwise I wouldn't be asking for the job," Fraser told her. "I've handled tough buckos before."

She was silent for a little time, her eyes big and dark with feeling. She faltered slightly when she spoke. "Sh— should any harm come to you after — after the kindness you've shown me! . . ."

"Now — now!" scoffed Nell Viney gently.

"Don't borrow trouble that may never show. You know we agreed that you couldn't hope to handle all the ranch affairs by yourself; that you needed a man to help you. In which case, where a better one that the one right before you? Also, as the pair of you will be working together, this stiffly formal Mister and Miss talk tries my withered soul. For goodness sake, make it Orde and Julie!"

The girl came before Fraser, slim and straight and still, her glance very direct. It was, he decided, as though she would read his every intent and thought beyond any mistake. Quickly her glance turned warm as she nodded and held out her hand.

"It's a bargain." Softly she added, "Be very careful, Orde! . . ."

When Fraser returned to Dan Larkin's office he found the marshal laying out a sawed-off double shotgun and a handful of brass-cased cartridges on his desk. His next move was to take off his badge of office and drop it into a desk drawer. Watching, Fraser made curt demand.

"And just what does all this mean?"

"Why," Larkin said with a small, grim smile, "it means that I'm taking a ride."

"A ride! When?"

"Tonight," said Larkin smoothly. "I often take a night ride."

Fraser shook his head. "Obliged, Dan — but not tonight and not with me," he said gruffly.

"Oh, yes — tonight, and with you," Larkin said, still smiling slightly. "Any time a young, upstart friend of mine aims to go spit in the devil's eye, I find I have to go along to see him do it." Glimpsing the stubborn resistance building in Fraser's glance, he added, "Use your head, son. I admit you're a real solid character in any kind of ruckus, but still and all you're just one man. And when you're heading into strictly enemy country, you need somebody to watch your back." Dan Larkin patted the sawed-off buckshot gun on the desk. "And there ain't anything in the world like a big, ten-gauge Greener like this one when it comes to cooling off a bunkhouse full of tough characters. Besides all that, there are some other angles to consider."

Larkin began pocketing the shotgun shells, then offered further argument.

"Not all of the present Rolling C crew are Turk Roderick's faithful ones. A few old-timers still hanging on out there rode for the outfit when Buckley Christiansen was alive, and who watched Julie Christiansen grow up. They've taken a lot of mean rawhiding from Roderick and his crowd, but they've kept their mouths shut, working hard and faithfully, waiting and hoping for a better day. None of them were in town the night you tangled with Roderick and Shep Riley was dragged; or along with Roderick when he pulled his other deviltry of burning out the little outfits. I know those men and they know me. They see me with you, they'll back your hand. And later you'll be able to use them in getting Rolling C off to a new start. That's the picture, son. Well? . . ."

The wisdom of this rugged old law man was beyond argument. Fraser shrugged, nodding. "You win, Dan."

CHAPTER XI

It was a night when several men would be out and riding in the star-shot dark beneath the frowning face of the great, black rim. One of them was a cowhand named Loop Vanner. Midway through the evening he stood at Pete Eagle's Ten High Bar, working at a couple of glasses of whiskey and a makeshift sandwich of beef and bread from Pete's free lunch shelf. Seeming concerned only with the food and drink before him, he still missed no move of the players at the poker table in the far corner.

Particularly did his narrow-lidded glance sharpen when Orde Fraser cashed in his stack of chips, left the game and the table and went on into the street. Now Loop Vanner's head lifted slightly and he listened intently. So it was that when the sudden, hard-blasting rumble of gunfire tore the night apart, Loop Vanner was among the first out into the street and part of the quick-gathering crowd around the sprawled figure of Rube Yard. There he heard what passed between Orde Fraser and Marshal Dan Larkin at the lantern-lit scene. Immediately thereafter he slipped quietly out of town and headed for Rolling C headquarters, riding hard.

Reaching there he left his blowing, sweating horse with a swinging leap and hurried into the ranch office. Here, where a lamp burned palely, Turk Roderick sat alone with whiskey bottle and glass. At Loop Vanner's entrance he came eagerly to his feet.

"How was it, Loop — how did Rube make out?"

"He didn't," reported Vanner tersely. "Rube Yard is dead. He had first bite and missed at less than fifteen feet. Fraser didn't miss!"

Mumbling a single searing curse, Turk Roderick dropped back in his chair and hunched there in glowering silence. As was always so with him, frustration turned him sullen and savage with an anger that congested his eyes, bulged the cords of his bull-like throat and pulled the heavy angles of his face into cruel and bitter lines. When he finally spoke, his words fell thick and heavy.

"So he had his good chance and missed twice at fifteen feet. And so now he's dead. The fool — the stupid, bumbling fool! . . ."

Such was the epitaph of Rube Yard. . . .

Moving to the door, Loop Vanner paused for his say. "Some people are the lucky ones. Born that way, seems like. Always things break right for them. Me, I see one of the lucky ones in that fellow Fraser. On top of luck he also shapes up as a plenty tough customer in his own right. So I want no part of any further ruckus with him. I don't usually make out to give free advice, but I'm saying this to you, Turk. You want a rough job done right, the only way to make sure is do it yourself!"

So saying, Loop Vanner left to unsaddle and corral his horse, then seek his own comfort in the bunkhouse.

Scorched by the raw fury of his mood, Turk Roderick let Loop Vanner's departing words register only at the outer fringe of his attention. But there they clung and their meaning now began to filter deeper. Presently, Roderick was considering them more carefully and in the doing of this knew a quickening purpose.

Hell, yes — Loop was right! Rube Yard was now dead. Ike Britt, full-fed and rested, was again on the prowl back in the Shoshone Lake country, intent on another try at skulking murder. But Britt had missed one try at Poe Darby, and the way the luck was breaking, might very well miss again. . . .

And Rube Yard — that impossible, bumbling fool. Hidden out just right, but advertising his presence by sucking on a cigarette! Even so, he had first bite at fifteen feet and wasted two shots. At Fraser — the big one — the one who counted more than anyone else. Before Fraser stepped off the Iron Mountain stage, all things had been going right. Since then, all things had gone wrong. Fraser — the name seemed a set echo in Turk Roderick's ears! . . .

Driven by the lash of his thoughts, Roderick got to his feet and to the door, there to stare

out at the night and the great rampart of the
rim reared against the night sky. In some
strange way he couldn't begin to analyze, sight
of the rim at night always awakened a sense of
power in Turk Roderick. He felt that power
now and it begot a renewed surge of confidence. All this country was his country. He
knew it forward and backward and the Shoshone Lake range was a vital and important
part of it. And no damned outsider like this
fellow Fraser was going to take it away from
him! He'd see to that himself, not leave it to
somebody else — not to anybody else like that
blundering fool of a Rube Yard. . . .

Twenty minutes later Turk Roderick was out
and riding, keeping well east of the town trail,
aiming for a wide swing that would bring him
up beyond the Shoshone Lake line cabin, so he
might work in on it from the blind side. A pair
of rolled-up blankets and a small sack of food
rode behind his saddle cantle. A scabbarded
Winchester slanted under his near saddle
fender.

In Humboldt City, beat down by a long and
momentous day, Benny Rust was about to cook
up a late supper in his cubby living quarters
next to his harness room. He had just set a pot
of coffee on to brew when a horse came into
the stable runway with the slack, dragging gait
that told of many weary miles left behind. Mut-
tering peevishly to himself Benny got his lan-

tern and went out there, sending an aggravated call well ahead.

"All right — who is it? Name yourself!"

"Jennette," came the answer. "Loan me the lantern, Benny, and I'll care of my horse myself."

Lifting the lantern high, Benny saw in Starr Jennette the gaunt and seedy look of a man who had been trying to escape his lonely thoughts by riding far and aimlessly, sleeping on the ground, going without regular food and rest. Reading these signs, Benny remarked on them.

"Man, you look plumb dragged out. What you been doin'?"

Deep-shadowed eyes pinched and frowning, Jennette had no immediate answer. It was as though he was trying to reason something out and then sneak it just right.

"Mainly only chasing my shadow down some interesting trails."

All of which failed to satisfy Benny's bump of curiosity. However, before he could inquire further, the pot of coffee he'd just put on began to steam and spread a warm fragrance into the wider space of the stable runway. Benny did not miss the quick, hungry lift of Starr Jennette's head.

"When," demanded Benny, "did you eat last?"

Jennette's twisted smile was thin and mirthless. "Really eat, you mean? Can't rightly remember. Earlier today I figured on a good meal at Swede Soderman's place at Hayfork Crossing. No luck. Wasn't any room for me there."

"No room for you?" exclaimed Benny, bewildered. "I can't figger that."

Jennette shrugged. "Forget it. I'll make out."

"Ain't about to forget it," returned Benny stoutly. "Hell, man — you got to eat. It's too late for a supper at the hotel and by now Pete Eagle's free lunch shelf will be worked bare. So you're eatin' with me. I got some good ham steaks and plenty of fried spuds to go with 'em. You will be more than welcome, Starr. I'm kinda low tonight and needin' some company."

"You — low? What about?" Jennette's glance was quick and keen.

"Lot of things," grumbled Benny. "I'm a peaceful man, liking life quiet and regular. This country used to be reasonable peaceful. But no more. Now there's seven different kinds of hell bustin' loose. Dead men in the street and all that sort of thing."

Pulling his thoughts back to supper, Benny handed his lantern to Jennette. "If'n we're to eat full and decent I got to get some biscuits in the oven. Put up your bronc. Grain him good, too. I can't stand havin' a honest horse facin' a hungry night." So saying, Benny scuttled back to his kitchen.

Finished caring for his horse, Starr Jennette washed up at the pump by the watering trough, dried himself on his faded neckerchief bandana and stepped into Benny Rust's kitchen. Here, empty flour sack tied at his rotund middle, Benny had a bottle and was pouring a stiff drink for his guest and a shorter one for himself.

He lifted his glass.

"Luck, Starr!"

Jennette put his drink away with a keen relish, then quietly spoke. "Benny, you're one damned good man!"

Benny squirmed under the praise. "Just a fat old stablehand who likes people and horses, that's me. And speaking personal, I allus need a second drink to hold the first one down."

Over this one it was Jennette who lifted his glass. "To you, Benny. Some day I'll square it all."

Benny waved a hand. "Just watchin' a hungry man enjoyin' his grub is enough for me. So sit up and dig in."

There was only one chair, but an empty horseshoe keg with a gunnysack folded on top of it, served as a second seat. Jennette went at his food with an absorption Benny did not interrupt. Done finally, Jennette sighed deeply, leaned back and reached for a smoke.

"Now I'm human again. And what's all this about dead men in the street? I know Shep Riley was dragged out there. You mean there was something else?"

Benny bobbed his head. "Not more'n a couple hours ago. Rube Yard was hid out, layin' for that new feller, Orde Fraser. Now Rube's in Wash Butterfield's warehouse, dead as he'll ever be."

"You mean — Fraser gunned him?"

"That's it," Benny said, warming to his subject. "Rube missed twice at real close range. But Fraser didn't. Dan Larkin said it was open and shut self-defense. Me, I'm sure glad it turned out like it did, because I like Orde Fraser. He's a good man."

Starr Jennette's eyes pinched down and his tone turned dry. "Capable, too — apparently."

"Darn right!" Benny emphasized. "Somethin' the Rolling C gang are due to find out, now that he's ridin' boss out there."

Jennette started, quickly intent. "What's that — what's that? Did you say Fraser was riding boss at Rolling C?"

"Sure did." Benny nodded, starting to clear away the dishes.

Leaning slowly back, Starr Jennette began twisting up another smoke. "Seems I've been missing many things. Suppose you tell me about them?"

Stuffed to the ears with news, this suited Benny right down to the ground. He drew a deep breath and went at it, telling how Julie Christiansen had fired Turk Roderick and when she went out to the ranch to take over, Roderick was there to defy her. And how, in the argument that followed, Julie had to throw a gun on Roderick to keep him in his place.

At this point, Starr Jennette hauled his head and shoulders up very straight and a strange, cold, faraway look came into his eyes.

Going ahead with his story, Benny told how he and Nell Viney drove out there and arrived just in time to keep matters from getting further out of hand; how they brought Julie back to town with her and Nell Viney talking things out and, at Nell Viney's urging, Julie agreeing to offer Orde Fraser the riding boss job. How Fraser first refused, but changed his mind after the shootout.

"Tell you somethin' else," Benny added. "The Rolling C crowd will sure know somebody has arrived when Fraser and Dan Larkin ride in out there tonight. When they came down here after their horses, both had their belt guns: Fraser his Winchester and Dan Larkin a big old sawed-off buckshot gun. Both of them had the cold business-look about 'em. So the fur is sure to fly at Rolling C!"

"Would seem so," murmured Jennette dryly. "How do you figure Larkin going along with Fraser? Dan's got no authority outside town."

Benny shrugged. "Dan's old and wise enough to know what he's doin'. And packin' that buckshot gun I'd say he had plenty of authority along."

"Once more, Benny," Jennette asked, "did Julie really have to put a gun on Turk Roderick to keep him in his place?"

"She sure enough did," vowed Benny. "When

I and Nell Viney got there, Julie was cryin' like a scared little kid as she crawled into Nell's arms."

Starr Jennette got to his feet. "That," he said gently, "I will remember. It seems, Benny, that the weeds are full of slickery ones. Who will also be remembered. You think there's any chance for me to see Henry Greer tonight?"

Benny pursed thoughtful lips before nodding. "You might at that. Henry is a book-readin' man. Never cottoned to books myself. Mebbe that is the reason he's a banker while I'm just a stablehand. Molly Dobbins, where he rooms, says at times Henry will sit up plumb past midnight, his nose in a book. Why don't you go see? Now there's somethin' else. I don't know where you figger to sleep tonight, but there's a spare bunk in my harness room. Ain't any fancy layout, but a heap better than sleepin' on the ground. You're welcome to use it."

"Which I'll do, with thanks. More and more I'm in your debt, Benny. Now I'll try my luck with Henry Greer."

A widow woman, Molly Dobbins's modest little cottage stood a short distance west of the courthouse. Henry Greer's room was an outside one with a separate door, so that he could come and go at his own convenience. There was a light gleaming in the room and at Starr Jennette's knock, Henry Greer opened the door.

"Yes? Who is it?"

"Starr Jennette, Mr. Greer. Wonder could I have a few minutes of your time?"

Ever a kindly man, Henry Greer was cordial. "Of course. Come right in."

He waved Jennette to a chair, then resumed his own by a table which held the lamp and a book turned face down. Over steel-rimmed spectacles he looked at Jennette. "What is it, Starr? Finances, perhaps?"

Jennette shook his head. "Nothing like that, sir. I'm concerned about certain people and what they may have in mind. Mr. Greer, what's your opinion of this new fellow, Orde Fraser?"

Henry Greer steepled his fingertips for a thoughtful moment before speaking past them. "The man seems personable enough. Capable too, apparently. I understand that Julie Christiansen has hired him on as riding boss in place of Turk Roderick. You knew of that?"

"Just learned of it," Jennette said. "And one of the reasons I've come to see you. Being a banker, you've probably heard of another named Blackwell?"

Sagging at ease in his chair, Henry Greer straightened quickly. "Indeed I have. Long Les Blackwell. Big man in banking. In cattle, too. Why do you mention him?"

"Because," Jennette said, speaking slowly to make his words more emphatic, "of talk I've heard and things I've seen out at Hayfork Crossing."

"Hayfork Crossing — Hayfork Crossing,"

frowned Henry Greer. "Oh, yes, now I recall it. That old stage stop between here and the Owyhee country. What about it, Starr?"

"I just came from there, sir. Right now there is upward of fifteen hundred head of Blackwell-owned cattle bunched and feeding on the east end of Rolling C range out back of Hayfork Crossing. They were brought in from the Owyhee country by a real bully boy named Carlin — Fitch Carlin. I understand he's the all-around big, bad, chore-boy for this fellow Blackwell, and the word is that when Blackwell is pointing to push somebody else to the wall, Carlin is the one who carries the cards. So I'm wondering what's to be done about those cattle on Rolling C range, and why they are there? Particularly since Julie Christiansen has just made that fellow Fraser her riding boss. Now I knew old Buck Christiansen quite well, Mr. Greer. And I remember one day hearing Buck Christiansen say something about a ruckus of some sort he'd had with a banker named Blackwell. And now, with Buckley Christiansen dead, I'm wondering, Mr. Greer — I'm wondering! . . ."

"When you put matters that way, so am I," said Henry Greer, visibly agitated. "It makes me recall this fellow Fraser, the morning after he arrived in town, coming into this bank to cash a draft of two thousand dollars, the draft drawn by Long Les Blackwell. Quite frankly, I wondered about it at the time, as I well remember the trouble that came up between Buckley Christiansen and Long Les Blackwell. It had to do over the very bank I now manage, and it built a strong, mutual animosity between the two men."

"So now," Jennette said bleakly, "we have this fellow Fraser laying claim to the Shoshone Lake range. Does it all mean to you, Mr. Greer, what it begins to mean to me?"

Leaving his chair, Henry Greer paced back and forth across the room, deep-held with sober, uneasy thoughts. "Starr," he said presently, "I am by nature and training a conservative man who tries to guard always against being guilty of snap judgement. At the same time, in my kind of business, it is ever wise to deal with facts, not theories. I believe I understand what is in your mind and must admit the logic of it. With Buckley Christiansen now dead and only a slip of a girl left to manage and handle Rolling C affairs, it would be quite a coup for Long Les Blackwell to move in on Rolling C, plus the Shoshone Lake range and add them to his already wide holdings. It could also satisfy Blackwell's ancient hate of Buckley Christiansen. Yes, indeed — quite a coup. At the same time I find it hard to believe that this man Fraser would be a willing partner to such a deal. Yet, who can guess what can go on in the mind of another human? . . . We must talk this over with Julie first thing in the morning!"

A deeply troubled man, Henry Greer moved

back and forth, murmuring to himself. "Poor Julie — poor girl! And what to do — What to do? . . ."

Starr Jennette stood up. "This is where I move into the game, Mr. Greer. I know I don't rate much in some ways, but in other ways I rate a hell of a lot!" Speaking, Jennette's hand brushed the gun at his hip. "Most generally there's one sure way of taking care of the Long Les Blackwells and the Orde Frasers of this world, and in that way I'm good — I'm damned good. So don't you worry, Mr. Greer. Just leave things to me. And you can believe me when I say that nobody — and I mean nobody — is going to give Julie Christiansen a bad time of it. Good night, Mr. Greer!"

Starr Jennette went out and moved quietly down the street. He paused in front of the hotel and for a little time stood looking up at it, lost in his deepest thoughts: brooding over what might have been, though now fully aware that it never could be. So, presently, he shook himself and went along to the stable to claim the bunk in Benny Rust's harness room.

CHAPTER XII

Riding out the dark miles, Orde Fraser and Dan Larkin pulled in beside the little creek that funneled off the rim past Rolling C headquarters and ran its moist, chuckling way through the willows at the foot of the slope. Dan Larkin waved an indicating hand.

"There it is, boy. Yonder is where you face up to the big chore. No light in the ranch house but plenty in the bunkhouse. Too damn much in the bunkhouse for this late at night when most honest cowhands would be in their blankets. Something has them all stirred up. Could it be, I wonder, that word of what happened to Rube Yard has already reached here?"

"Let's get up there and find out," Fraser said, swinging down. "We go in from here on foot."

They tied their horses in the willows and hung their spurs on their saddle horns. Fraser reached for the buckshot gun.

"My showdown, Dan. So I go in first with the Greener. The bargain was that you'd just keep them off my back."

"Right!" Larkin agreed. "But remember, at least three of the men up there are good men. Let me handle them."

They climbed the slope slowly, keening the

night at every step. On their left the ranch house bulked, dark and still. Dead ahead, the rim was its usual grim, shadowed self. The small night wind that slid off that massive wall and scurried down the hill brought with it the earthy odors of feed sheds and corrals. Also, on the night wind rode the pitchy fragrance of fat-pine wood smoke from the cook shack chimney. The bunkhouse door was open and from it was carried the growling voices of men in uneasy, desultory argument.

At Orde Fraser's shoulder, Dan Larkin murmured, "Go on in, boy, and lay it on the line. I'm right with you."

Just short of the outer edge of light from the bunkhouse door, Orde Fraser paused to cock both barrels of the shotgun. Then, with the gun at hip-high level, he took three quick strides and filled the doorway with cold threat and bitter words.

"Freeze — everybody! And let me see your hands!"

After the first explosive stir of startled movement, a long moment of breathless stillness held. From a dozen different angles and positions, men stared at Fraser and the gaping muzzles of the gun he held. Fraser broke the moment of stillness.

"Don't make me get any rougher about this deal than I want to. But I'm the new riding boss of this outfit, and from now on that is how it will be!"

Past Fraser's shoulder, Dan Larkin made quick call. "Barney Rawlins, Zeke Vale and Joe Thomas — take it easy. This showdown isn't aimed at you."

At the far end of the bunkhouse three men were already in their blankets. As one they came up on their elbows, staring. Out of a round, ruddy, button-nosed face half-shrouded in grizzled whiskers came a relieved laugh and rumbling words.

"Hello, Dan! You're welcome — and how! Zeke and Joe and me, we been waitin' and hopin' for something like this for a long time."

A short stride from Orde Fraser a roan-headed puncher made a quick half-turn, grabbing at a belt gun hanging from a wall peg.

"Not me, by God! . . ."

A roomful of men were in line had Fraser turned the roaring blasting fury of the big Greener gun loose. Instead he moved quickly ahead, swinging the snout of the gun up and driving the butt hard forward as the puncher came whirling back with his drawn gun. The heavy butt of the Greener drove into the side of his head, dropping him to the floor, senseless.

Bringing the Greener back level, Fraser laid out further harsh warning.

"Steady — all! Don't make me do that again. One fool is enough. Where's Turk Roderick?"

Sitting on the edge of his bunk, Loop Vanner had been stuffing odds and ends of personal gear into the warbag between his feet.

At Fraser's demand, he looked up.

"Pulled out a while ago. Took some blankets, a sack of grub and a Winchester. Like he aimed to make war some place." Vanner looked around at his fellow riders and laughed thinly. "Tried to tell you knotheads that the sun had gone down for us and we'd be smart to drift. Maybe you'll believe me, now." His glance touched the man sprawled at Fraser's feet. "That stupid jackass could have got us all filled with buckshot!" His glance lifted to Fraser again and he raised a hand in salute. "Many thanks, stranger, for not pulling the triggers of that cannon you're waving. I was dead in line."

Dan Larkin pulled a blanket off a bunk and made a pouch. "I'll be taking your guns," he said briskly. "You can have them back at my office tomorrow, in case you're interested. All right, now — one by one, hand them to me, butt first!"

He went down the length of the room, collecting. Fraser covered his progress, alert to any further show of hostility. There was none, the authority of the big shotgun was too awesome. Also, by this time the wisdom of Loop Vanner's words was taking effect.

"All right — I'm ready to pull out," said one of the crew. "But I got some legal wages comin' from this damn layout. How about them?"

"Anything you've full right to will be paid you by Henry Greer at the bank," Fraser told him. "Who knows where the time books are?"

"I do," Barney Rawlins said.

"Get them," Fraser ordered.

Barney was quickly up and into his clothes. He took a lantern off a wall peg and hurried out.

Dan Larkin spoke up. "Our horses are in the willows down slope. Joe, you go after them. Zeke, you comb the saddle shed for any long guns."

Joe Thomas and Zeke Vale were up and at it eagerly. Pausing for a moment, Zeke looked around and had his brief say. "This change of air suits me plumb across the boards. Now I can breathe decent again!"

Orde Fraser had blunt words for the rest of them. "Pack your gear — you're leaving us!"

Came grumbling complaint. "Where we sleepin' tonight?"

Fraser smiled thinly. "It's a big, wide world. Better men than you have slept out in the sage. That's how it is, so hurry it up!"

Came one further try at argument. "How do we know this ain't all a bluff? How do we know you got the authority to turn us out?"

Fraser pushed a boot toe against the man at his feet. "This look like a bluff? As for authority, there's more of this!" He jammed the muzzle of the shotgun into the belly of the doubter. "Now I'm tired of talk. You're all traveling. You can take your gear or leave it behind!"

The touch of a boot toe had brought movement from Red Lubin, the man on the floor. He rolled over, pushed up slightly, groaned and fell back again. Fraser was remorseless.

"Put him on a bunk. When you leave, saddle a horse for him, too."

Someone said, "Red's in no shape to travel. What kind of an Indian are you, anyhow?"

"The kind all you brave buckos were set to gang up on the first night I arrived in town," Fraser retorted. "Now it's my turn — yeah, my turn. And I'm calling it!"

It was Turk Roderick who had built up this crew and held them together with a rough, heavy-handed authority. It was Roderick who had done the thinking, called the turns and plotted the moves. But Roderick wasn't around now and they didn't know where he was or what he was about. For all they knew, he might have left the country. All they were sure of right now was this cold-eyed man with the shotgun, and the fact that Dan Larkin was backing his hand. Earlier, Loop Vanner had brought word of the violent finish of Rube Yard. Now, finished packing his warbag, it was Loop Vanner who stood up, ready to go and saying so.

"No argument here. Come on — come on, you damned fools. This man means business! . . ."

There was no further delay. Hurriedly they collected their gear.

Zeke Vale came in with three rifles, which he stacked in a corner. "All there were in the saddle shed," he reported. "Might be a couple more over in the office."

Joe Thomas came in out of the night. "Horses ready and waitin', Dan."

Fraser handed the shotgun to Larkin. "Keep an eye on things. I want a little talk with our three friends. Come on, Joe — Zeke."

He led them across to the ranch office where Barney Rawlins was just about to leave. Fraser drew them inside.

"Knowing this whole deal could turn up real rough and dirty at any time, I want to make sure you men mean to stay on. How about it?"

"Already had my say," put in Zeke Vale quickly. "I'm sure Joe and Barney feel the same. Hell, man! We rode for this outfit when old Buck Christiansen was alive and we watched Julie grow up — half-raised her, you could say. We took considerable pushin' around by Turk Roderick and his crowd, but we hung on, waitin' and hopin' for a change. Now that it's come, we're not about to fold. We're here, solid, come what may!"

"Just so," affirmed Barney. The glance he showed Fraser was direct and steady. "You don't let us down, we won't let you down."

"Which makes it a bargain," Fraser said. "For a time you three men will be running the ranch by yourselves. Soon as I can, I'll round up some more good hands. Meantime, should Turk Roderick or any of his pet crowd try coming back, throw a couple of slugs their way, because they're definitely all through here.

Something more. When they begin saddling up, see that they take only what they've a right to."

"Count on it," Barney promised. "One more thing. Smokie Gant is a good man and an old-timer here, same as us three. He took his share of rawhidin' from Roderick same as we did, not likin' it any better, either. On top of that, he's the best damn cook this side the rim."

"Good enough!" Fraser said. "Glad you spoke up. Smokie Gant stays on."

Things moved quickly after that. Horses were caught up and saddled, operations carefully checked by Barney Rawlins and the other two faithful. Barney had a lantern in each hand, Zeke and Joe, handy and watchful, had rifles across their arms. Red Lubin, still rocky and shambling, was helped out to the corrals and boosted into a saddle, where he humped low, both hands clutching the horn. After having a look, Barney shook his head.

"Long night comin' up for Red Lubin."

"No tears here," declared Zeke Vale. "Asked for it, didn't he? Me, I sure go for the style of our new boss. I can follow a man like that."

The pace Orde Fraser and Dan Larkin set on their way back to town was leisurely, and the dark they traveled through was deep and chill and silent. By the slant of the stars, Dan Larkin figured the night was well along, a fact to be re-marked on lugubriously.

"Been a considerable chore, with morning coming on fast. Me, I'm feeling my years.

When I do hit the blankets I'll be real annoyed at anybody who comes bothering too early."

Fraser grinned into the darkness. "Feel some that way myself. While trying to think up the proper words of thanks, Dan."

Larkin snorted. "No thanks necessary. You should know that."

By the time they reached town, cared for their horses and sought their respective beds, the first faint seep of gray dawn light was stealing in across the eastern edge of the world.

Out at Shoshone Lake, two other men were astir in that gray dawn. Turk Roderick lay out behind the east end of the low lava spine that curved below the line cabin. From this spot the lake trail was only a fair shot away for a man who had a solid rest for his rifle and who took time and care enough to make sure of his target. When Orde Fraser next came to the line camp it would be along that trail. So now it was just a matter of wait and watch until the big chance offered.

Roderick knew Ike Britt was on the prowl and there was always the chance of him getting to Fraser first along some other stretch of trail, but there was no certainty about it. Hell — no! Hadn't he counted on Rube Yard? And Rube, the stupid, fumbling clod, with all the breaks in his favor, had bungled things and now lay dead for it, back in town. So it was as Loop Vanner had said, when bringing word of Rube's blundering failure. "The only sure way to get a thing done, was do it yourself." That was what Loop Vanner had said, and he was right!

The waiting wasn't easy, and Roderick felt the full effects of the night he'd put in at a siwash camp some three miles back in the sage. The ground had been hard, the night cold, and sleep little and sketchy. The cold food he'd eaten now lay heavy in his belly and at the moment he would have traded a year of his life for a couple of good stiff jolts of whiskey and a hot cup of coffee. But neither was to be had and it was still too dark to see any distance with clarity, so now he lay back to try and catch up on some of the rest he'd missed out on, back in the sage.

Just at this time, over at the cabin, Poe Darby eased through the door and kenned the awakening world round about like a wary old wolf. He had his rifle across his arm and presently he stole off, circling the west edge of the lake with such noiseless care he passed within five short yards of a resting plover without disturbing it.

Well out in the vicinity of the tall tule growth from which had come a treacherous shot on an earlier day, he found a spot to his liking. Here he settled down in the marsh growth to wait and watch while the world came fully awake.

In the far distance a lone coyote mourned the end of another night of hunting. Closer at hand a beef critter bawled its restless hunger. All about the lake there came the quickening stir of awakening life, sensed rather than seen or

213

heard. Against the eastern sky a band of silver light grew broader and brighter.

All were sights and sounds Poe Darby had known many times before and he noted them now with an unconscious perception that came to him as naturally as the act of breathing. Ordinarily he would have savored them deeply and at length, for such were the things that ever nourished him and made his world great. At the moment, however, they were neither the sounds nor sights he waited and hoped for.

Darkly brooding, he wondered if he had figured his moves soundly. Perhaps the man he waited for was smarter than he thought. Still and all, the only place this side of the lake offering real concealment close enough for a reasonably certain rifle shot was right here, with its thick growth of tules. Also, for all his heavy brutishness, there was in Ike Britt an animal slyness. It would be like him to reason in this manner. No one would expect him to return to the identical spot for a second try at stealthy murder, so that was the very place he would select. That was how Poe Darby had decided and why he was here, waiting. . . .

Steadily the dawn sky brightened and a visual tide that was half-light and half-dark flowed across the world. Now, with full dawn only minutes away, growing doubt of his strategy held Poe Darby. It had been, he decided a little wearily, a long gamble at best, and long gambles did not pay off very often. . . .

He was about to rise from his crouched rest when out there, at no great distance, a startled plover winged into flight, crying out its thin plaint of alarm. Immediately after, along the sounding board of the earth came the pace of muffled hoofs and a mounted figure shaped against the brightening sky.

Though still too shadowy to clearly distinguish facial features, the thick, squat bulk of the rider was identification enough for Poe Darby. Also, as was always the case in situations of this sort, there was an instinctive ripple of feeling up Poe's spine which he had come to trust as much or more than what he saw or didn't see. So, rifle ready, he stepped fully into the clear and hit out with blunt, hard challenge.

"Back for another sneak try, eh Britt? Aiming to play it real sly. Well, I figgered you likely would — so now comes payoff! . . ."

Poe's Winchester came to his shoulder, leveled, and deadly. The gust of startled breath that broke from Ike Britt's throat was an eruptive rasp as he tried to haul his horse up and around. But well ahead of this move, the hard blast of Poe's rifle flung a pounding echo rocketing up at a shocked sky and across the roundabout world.

Startled into flight, a long skein of blackbirds that had roosted for the night on the massed tips of the tule clumps winged into flight with a sibilant rushing, and all along the marshy lake borders killdeer plover were fleeing and crying.

Ike Britt's big black horse was quickly fifty yards away, snorting and stamping under an empty saddle. Swinging the lever of his rifle, Poe Darby jacked a fresh cartridge from magazine to chamber and paced grimly forward through dawn's quickening light to where a motionless figure was flung against the patient earth. Poe had his look, then spoke his bitter, unforgiving thoughts.

"Ike Britt, you were a dirty, damn dog, and you died too quick and easy. For you deserved some of what Shep Riley went through while dragging at the end of your rope. Now you'll never harm another good man, and I'll sleep the better, knowing I was the one who pulled trigger on you!"

The reins that had slithered from Ike Britt's dead fingers had grounded, so that his horse, though still chuffing and swinging nervously back and forth, was holding true to the tie, and Poe was able to reach the reins and draw the horse along behind him as he headed back for the cabin. Andy Quider, showing open relief, met him at the door.

"Heard the shot," Andy said. "Worried some, wondering about it. Ike Britt, of course?"

"Just so," Poe nodded. "He came back to the bait he missed before, just like we figgered he might. Some diggin' to do now, Andy. Any tools around?"

"Couple of old ones. Shep Riley must have used them to deepen the spring out back. But me, I'm not diggin' anything anywhere until we've grubbed. You up to eatin' breakfast?"

"Hell, yes — of course I am," snorted Poe. "All I did was rid the world of a two-legged sidewinder who was out to shoot some better man in the back. I've felt far worse having to put an honest, but maybe crippled horse out of its misery."

When the ringing crash of Poe Darby's rifle rocketed across the Shoshone Lake world, Turk Roderick was slacked down behind the lava spine, near to dozing off after his sleepless night. Instantly wide awake now, he lunged to the lava crest, staring off toward the lake and the cabin and the dim world beyond still held in early morning mists. At first he could see nothing out of the ordinary until, well out past the lake's western shore where the tule growth was thick and high, came movement that resolved into a man carrying a rifle and leading a horse.

The man with the rifle was Poe Darby and the horse he led was a rangy black with a blaze face and white points: a horse that was suddenly and strikingly familiar to Turk Roderick. When and where had he last seen that horse? Yesterday, it was — yesterday! Out at Rolling C headquarters, when Ike Britt rode that horse up to the corrals and stepped down from the now-empty saddle! . . .

But now it was Poe Darby leading the animal toward the line camp cabin. And with the saddle empty, where was Ike Britt? There had

been a single crashing rifle shot, and now —
this! . . . There could be only one answer. In
town, Rube Yard had blundered and died for it.
Out here, Ike Britt had blundered, and died for
it. . . .

Black, bitter fury convulsed Turk Roderick.
Plans, plans, plans — and all going wrong! Out
there now, Poe Darby was within fair range and
Roderick brought his rifle up, half-leveled it.
Then caution whispered and he lowered the
gun. Poe Darby didn't really count. Fraser was
the only one who really counted. Fraser,
Fraser, Fraser — the name hammered at
Roderick's mind. But now another thought in-
truded. What was it Loop Vanner had said
about Orde Fraser? Vanner had said that Fraser
was one of the lucky ones, for whom all things
seemed to break favorably. And you couldn't,
according to Loop Vanner's reasoning, beat a
lucky man.

The edge of doubt and sense of aloneness
that had punished him during the past long
and, for him, miserable night now came back
over Turk Roderick with double the force. With
it also came the weight of questions — what to
do — what to do — where to turn? . . . To cut
down on Poe Darby now would prove nothing,
solve nothing. Least of all would it bring Ike
Britt back. . . .

Alone — alone! Of a sudden all Turk
Roderick wanted to do was get away — far
away, where he might pull his thoughts together

and figure a new set of plans. Such a refuge could be neither Humboldt City nor Rolling C headquarters. Instead, let it be some place where he might find good food, good liquor and a decent bed for the night. Such a place could be Swede Soderman's layout at Hayfork Crossing. Keeping well behind the lava spine, Turk Roderick headed for his horse.

For Poe Darby and Andy Quider it had come up midmorning before their digging chore was done. The spot was well away from the lake's border. Spreading a last shovel of earth on the long, narrow mount, Andy took his usual alert look around and came up straight, exclaiming.

"Somebody ridin' in at the cabin. Looks like Hollis Ward. Now what would he be wantin' out here?"

"Whatever it is, he's welcome," grunted Poe. "Always liked Hollis. Let's get back there."

The old cattleman was out of his saddle and hunkered on his heels in the sun beside the cabin door when they came up. He gave them his faded glance and murmured a quiet show of grim humor. "Would you boys been burying something — treasure, maybe?"

"Just so," Poe said succinctly. "Ike Britt."

Hollis Ward's wrinkled cheeks pulled taut. "Devil, you say! Ike Britt? You buried him?"

"That's it," Poe said. "And I've helped bury better men."

Hollis Ward considered, then nodded soberly. "I can agree with that. How did it happen?

219

What's that scum been doing around here?"

"Hopin' to gulch somebody. Made a try at it yesterday morning, but missed. You can see the bullet hole in the wall just above your head. Andy and me, we figgered he'd probably be back for another try. Which he was. And I was layin' for him. He'll never gulch another man, Hollis — or drag one to death, either."

Hollis Ward's faded glance had sharpened as he listened. "And it accounts for the second of the bad ones. Things are happening, men — things are happening."

"What things you talkin' about, Hollis?" demanded Andy Quider. "And what two bad ones? Who's the other one?"

"Rube Yard," said Hollis Ward with obvious relish. "In town last night. He made a try for Orde Fraser from the dark, but his luck ran out. So Rube's no longer with us. Also, the word is that Julie Christiansen has sure enough fired Turk Roderick and hired Orde Fraser on in his place as riding boss of Rolling C. So things are looking better all the time."

Held in shrewd speculation over this information, Poe Darby got out his pipe, packed it and ran a flaming match back and forth across the bowl. He made each move mechanically, for his thoughts were grim and elsewhere. Presently, he cleared his throat harshly.

"Turk Roderick may be through at the Christiansen ranch, but long as he's loose and runnin' free, nothin' is sure or settled. . . ."

CHAPTER XIII

A man of habit at early rising, Orde Fraser rarely overslept. However, under the weight of a long day and equally long night of dangerous and at times savagely brutal activity, he did so on this particular morning. Sunlight was a streaming brilliance through his window when he awoke and Nell Viney's Rimview Hotel was held by a quiet at marked variance with its usual rustle of activity.

He wondered about this as he was swiftly up, dressed, washed and dropping downstairs. With usual breakfast time well past, the dining room was empty. Driven by eager hunger, he again invaded the kitchen territory. One of the Indian girls pointed to the corner table and put hot food in front of him. It was done without comment of any kind and when he caught her eye it seemed she was looking at him from a great distance.

Which was something else to wonder about and he finally concluded it had to be because of the Rube Yard affair. And though he had acted strictly in defense of his own life, the outcome could have placed a mark against him in the shy, gentle thoughts of this darkeyed Shoshone Indian girl. Because he had killed a man. . . .

There being nothing he could do about it now, he pushed the thought aside and ate hungrily. Finished with breakfast, he was building a brown paper cigarette when Nell Viney came into the room and faced him across the table with an expression that was at once stern, hostile, accusing and, strangely enough, almost tearful.

Fraser stared. Here again complete change from the usual. Unable to understand he made wondering demand. "What's wrong? Why the look of near-hating me and ready to cry about it? If it's because of the Rube Yard deal, you know I had no choice. It was him or me. I'm no way proud of the result, but what's done is done!"

Nell Viney gulped and her answer was muffled. "It has nothing to do with Rube Yard, who got what he deserved. It's the other thing that people are saying about you. And if it is true, I'll never trust another human being as long as I live! They are waiting for you over at the bank."

Quickly up and around the table, Fraser caught her by both arms and gave her a gentle shake. "Look at me! What's this nonsense about trust or no trust? What in blazes are you driving at? And just who is waiting for me over at the bank?"

"Julie Christiansen, Henry Greer and Starr Jennette," wailed Nell Viney. "And if you've double-crossed us and tricked me into helping swindle that poor girl, I'll never forgive myself or cease to hate you as long as I live!"

Fraser released her and stepped back, frankly bewildered. "This," he said bluntly, "I don't understand. I haven't the slightest idea what you are talking about. For your information, Nell Viney, I haven't double-crossed anybody that I know of. But if they are waiting for me, I'll oblige them. I'll go right over, as I've something for Henry Greer and something to say to all three!"

He went back upstairs, two at a time. He buckled on his gun, caught up his saddlebags and the time books he'd brought in from the ranch last night. Quickly back downstairs he found Nell Viney waiting for him in the lobby. She pointed at the saddlebags.

"Why those?"

"Because," he said bruskly, "I'm leaving. I never stay where I'm not wanted. Trot out my bill. What do I owe you?"

This gaunt, kindly woman, old enough to be his mother, had steadied down emotionally. Now she stepped up to him, reaching for the saddlebags. "Leave them here. And look at me, Orde Fraser — look at me! . . ."

Their glances met and held. The taut lines of Nell Viney's face relaxed and she nodded, as though what she had seen had convinced her of something.

"Forgive me, boy," she said simply. "I was wrong and they are wrong. Go tell them I said that! . . ."

Though regular opening time was a good hour away, the bank door swung freely under Orde Fraser's hand. They were there, all right, the three of them, gathered beyond the wicket. Starr Jennette straddled a chair, arms folded across the back of it. Henry Greer fidgeted nervously at the wicket window. Seated in a far corner, Julie Christiansen stared straight ahead at nothing.

Fraser's glance was harsh as it swept the room. "I was told you wanted to see me, so here I am. By the look of things you've decided to be judge and jury with some kind of loco verdict already arrived at on whatever it is that's bothering you. Nell Viney just gave me some talk about a double-cross being in progress. Apparently she could be right, with me the victim. She also said that she'd been wrong and that you three are wrong — and that I was to tell you so."

He tossed the time books in front of Henry Greer. "You could have use for these, as there may be some ex-Rolling C hands in to collect wages due them. I wouldn't know about that. But being a man of figures, you can take care of it."

He shifted his glance to Starr Jennette. "From all past words and opinions, garnered from here and there — including my own, perhaps mistakenly — I can't quite savvy you being in on anything like this. But as long as you are, let's hear from you. What do you know about a

224

double-cross? Speak up — speak up! . . ."

"Just so, I will," Jennette said smoothly. "First, I'd like to know if you are liar or fool, or both. Because right now there are a good fifteen hundred head or more of Long Les Blackwell cattle, just in from the Owyhee country, crowded onto Rolling C range, out at Hayfork Crossing. Also, there's a real tough segundo in charge — fellow named Fitch Carlin, backed by some tough hands. Finally, there's Long Les Blackwell on hand in person, apparently to oversee the big steal. Yeah, Long Les Blackwell, traveling in a shiny spring wagon with a special driver, a matched pair of thoroughbred gray trotting horses and all the comforts of home piled in back of the fancy rig. Just like he knew he was going somewhere and intending to stay there for a while. So now, Orde Fraser, suppose you tell us what you know about all these things?"

For a long moment Orde Fraser stood very still. Then his answer came quietly. "News to me — all of it."

"So you say," Jennette continued. "But you have to admit it makes a very peculiar picture — too much so to be shrugged aside. First, there is the way you came in across the rim, laying claim to the Shoshone Lake range. Then there was the item of a good-sized bank draft that you cashed right in this very room, a draft drawn up by none other than Long Les Blackwell. Oh, the draft was good, all right, being small price for what he figures to buy with it — which is Julie Christiansen's ranch.

"Pretty neat deal, you and Blackwell, working together. You taking over the Shoshone Lake range and making talk of cattle coming in to stock it, while knowing all the time that the herd coming in was to end up right where it is now — on Rolling C grass. Things really broke good for you, didn't they — what with people believing in you like they did. Even allowed you to move in as riding boss of Rolling C, which really stripped the deck. That had me, among others, fooled for a time!"

Cold-jawed, cold-eyed, Orde Fraser faced him, full of challenge. "Go ahead, swing the knife. Carve me up good, if you're enjoying it! Quite sure of all your talk, are you? Got it all figured out among yourselves? Well, let me put you right on a few things. Here's something for you to chew on. You've just made a lot of talk you'll be called on to prove — or eat! We'll let the tag of 'fool' stand, as it seems I've been a prime one, believing in people who don't believe in me. But the other tag — the 'liar' one — that one you'll eat, friend Jennette!"

He came around far enough to put his glance on Julie Christiansen. "For you, there are three good men, plus a cook, now holding things together out at your headquarters. The balance of the old crew, Turk Roderick and his pet outfit are all gone. Finally, I'm holding on to the job of your riding boss long enough to see every head of Blackwell cattle heading back to where it came from. After which I become my own man again, strictly! And I won't be double-crossing you or anyone else anymore." He made as if to turn away, then came back, his glance very direct, his voice going a little husky with feeling. "And I thought that you had grown up! . . ."

Now as he moved to the door, Starr Jennette was quickly out of his chair. "Just where do you think you're going?"

Fraser's answer was savagely cold, brittle as breaking ice. "Right now, none of your damned business, Jennette! And if you think you can stop me — have at it! Just for the record, so there'll be no more mistakes, I'm on my way to Hayfork Crossing to see about this double-cross business! . . ."

So saying, he was swiftly out and on his way down to the stable.

In the bank he left a girl who now came to her feet a little blindly. Her lips were twisted, her chin trembling, her words a choked wail. "He looked at m-me like I'd hit him across the face with a whip!" She began to sob brokenly. "An-and we're wrong. All of-of us — so very wrong. We — we are the f-fools — and so wrong — so wrong! . . ."

Henry Greer cleared an uncomfortable throat. "I must admit, those were neither the words nor actions of a guilty man! . . ."

Watching keenly, Starr Jennette marked Julie Christiansen's tears, and a shadow of regret darkened his own eyes. He tipped his head and made quiet statement.

"Could be I've got a lot of words to eat. If he's headed out to tangle with such as Fitch Carlin and Long Les Blackwell and company, then a fellow like me could come in handy. So I'll be there."

When Orde Fraser arrived at the stable, Benny Rust showed a reserved, somewhat distant front. Fraser hit out at him harshly.

"Now don't you start looking at me like I was something that just crawled out of a rotten log! Stir that fat carcass and bring my horse out here. Right now I can't get away from this damn town and the people in it quick enough!"

Benny's eyes bugged and he scuttled off at little less than a run. When he returned with the dun, Fraser did the saddling himself. He cracked the action of his rifle, then slid it back into the scabbard and hit out with further harsh words. "I want a good feed of oats for the dun. Sack it and bring it. Hustle!"

Benny hustled, then stood shifting uncomfortably from one foot to the other while Fraser tied the oat sack behind his saddle cantle. Swinging astride, Fraser looked down, marked the bare, forlorn misery in Benny's eyes and made his next remark a little kinder.

"If your feelings are hurt, Benny — just remember that mine are scraped raw! . . ."

He pulled the dun around and out into the street and there hauled up abruptly. For Julie

Christiansen was there looking up at him, tears leaking down her face. She had been running and her hair had loosened and fallen about her shoulders. She was panting and her words were stumbling and half-sobbing.

"Orde — Orde, I-I'm s-sorry — you can't leave me — this way! I was wrong — we were all of us wrong — all but you. And — and I have grown up. Orde, please — don't hate me — don't hate me! . . ."

Looking down at her, the brittle hardness that had been in his glance, in the curtness of his words and the set of his jaw, all relaxed and softened. He leaned down and ran a gentle fingertip across her cheeks, wiping away a smear of tears.

"Poor little worried, mixed-up kid! Me — hate you? Never in this world — or any other . . . . And I'll be back, Julie. That's a promise!"

She stood half on hesitant tiptoe, her hands clasped in front of her. Over and over she whispered his name. "Orde — Orde — be careful — please be careful! . . ."

Though he had left Shoshone Lake very shortly after the break of day, it was close to noon when Turk Roderick rode in at Hayfork Crossing on a horse gone dead lame because of a stone bruise picked up along the way. With him rode deepening depression, product of the abrupt collapse of his personal fortunes. All the great plans of a cattle empire were as nothing now, having gone sour on every side. And the two men he'd gambled on to carry out the more ugly, brutal angles of his scheme of conquest, Ike Britt and Rube Yard, were both dead.

At Hayfork Crossing Roderick found changes to startle and baffle him. After putting his limping mount up to Swede Soderman's hitch rail and dismounting there, he went still, listening. From beyond the buildings all the way to the upraised, heat-misted bulk of the Humboldt Rim ran a wide flat that was the eastern end of the Rolling C range. And right now, carrying in off that flat was the massed bovine complaint of harried cattle freshly arrived on new range and not yet settled down to peaceful grazing on it.

From his own present knowledge of Rolling C affairs, Roderick knew there were no Christiansen cattle on that piece of range just now. So why and where from the herd now occupying it? Wondering about this, he pushed through the door of Swede Soderman's dingy barroom.

Swede held his usual place behind the bar. Across the battered mahogany from him, three saddle hands fiddled over their drinks. At a poker table farther along, two other men sat, bottle and glasses beside them as they conversed in low tones. But as Roderick entered, all heads turned and all talk turned quiet. Seeking a place at the bar, Roderick gestured for a drink. Swede poured it, watched Roderick down it at a gulp, then refilled the glass

Roderick pushed toward him. Noting Turk Roderick's seedy appearance, Swede murmured cautiously, "Long ride, Turk, maybe?"

"Long enough," Roderick nodded. "And I could stand a good meal."

Swede started for the rear door. "I'll go tell Sophie."

Roderick dawdled over his second drink, trying to work out some answers. Because there was something loose in this room, a sense of guarded suspicion, an edge of strain. Reaching for the cause, Roderick made a slow turn, putting his shoulders against the bar, sipping at his drink while laying his glance here and there past the run of his glass. All present were total strangers to him. The three men at the bar seemed ordinary saddle hands. But the two men at the poker table were no part of ordinary.

One was inordinately tall and thin, with high-pointed shoulders, a bony, narrow-angled face and a head of bushy white hair which gave an impression of benevolence. It was an impression quickly dissipated for Roderick when he met a pair of slightly hooded eyes as black and hard and shiny as flecks of obsidian. Strange eyes, shrewd and cold and calculating. Below a hungry beak of a nose, the mouth was small and tight and thin of lip. All in all, Roderick decided in swift judgement, a man to beware of, a man who was dangerous.

The second man at the poker table was also

high-shouldered, but heavy of build. His hair was sandy, his face round and broad with flat, coarse features and a pair of murky eyes set so far apart as to give his stare a studied, repulsive, frog-like effect. Turk Roderick was wondering and guessing at the close, hard scrutiny these two at the poker table were sending his way, so he knew a sense of relief when Swede came and called.

"Sophie's got your grub ready."

Sophia Soderman was completely out of sorts. The pert, tidy little lady was completely fed up with men and their doings. The usual easy pace of the days at Hayfork Crossing had, in the past thirty hours, been completely shattered. The place was overrun with swaggering, spur-dragging saddle hands smelling of cattle dust, horse and human sweat; guzzling whiskey, demanding more and more in the way of food, offending her ears with loud and boisterous talk until she was ready to unearth Swede's old shotgun and go on a rampage of her own.

She eyed Turk Roderick with no friendliness at all and by her look, silently dared him to say one word against her cooking. She could have saved the thought, for it was the best food Roderick had tasted in weeks and he dug into it voraciously.

When Swede Soderman returned to the barroom the tall, thin man at the poker table caught his eye and gave a beckoning nod. Swede knew who this man was all right. And he didn't like any part of Long Les Blackwell. Nor did he care for Fitch Carlin, the froggy-eyed one who was with Blackwell at the poker table. But Swede was a man of peace, so now, under the weight of their demanding stares, he moved over to their table.

"Who," Blackwell demanded, "is that fellow you're feeding?"

"That's Turk Roderick," informed Swede. "Used to be riding boss of Rolling C. But according to the word leakin' out of Humboldt City, it seems Buck Christiansen's daughter, having taken over at the ranch, just fired Roderick. I don't know nothin' for sure about that, but it's what I've heard."

"Well — well," murmured Blackwell, "Ex-foreman of Rolling C, eh? Sounds interesting. When he's done feeding, tell him I want to see him."

Swede delivered the word, then ducked out into the street, to get away from the tension in the barroom and get some cleaner air into his lungs.

When Turk Roderick returned to the barroom he was twisting up a cigarette. He paused to lick it into shape, light it and savor the first draw or two. After which he crossed to the poker table. Long Les Blackwell lifted an acknowledging hand.

"Drag up a chair. I'm Les Blackwell. This is my riding boss, Fitch Carlin. Understand you used to ride for the Christiansen interests. If it's that way, maybe we could do a little business."

Roderick took another drag at his cigarette, his eyes veiling. "What kind of business?"

"Like this," Long Les said smoothly. "Having ridden for the Christiansen outfit, you must know considerable about its affairs. Where all its range runs, a fair guess at the number of cattle packing the Christiansen iron, general state of finances — all that sort of thing. I can use such information and I'm willing to pay for it. What say?"

For a little time Turk Roderick sat silent, frowning his thoughts. A shadowed gleam sparked far back in his eyes, took form and grew. Here was a chance to get even all along the line. He looked up with quickening interest.

"Suits me. We can make a deal."

Out in the street sounded the mutter of arriving hoofs, and Swede Soderman watched Orde Fraser ride in. Swede exclaimed his pleasure.

"Mister Fraser! What brings you here?"

"People-hunting, Swede," Fraser said tersely. "Any around?"

Swede nodded toward the door of his barroom. "Some, in there."

"Would one be named Blackwell — Long Les Blackwell?"

"Him and the bad one, Fitch Carlin. Turk Roderick just showed up a little bit ago, too. You want to see them?"

"Yes, Swede — I want to see them — all!"

The way he said it, the way he looked, gave Swede Soderman a strong hint of what was in Orde Fraser's mind and what his purpose might be. So now Swede proffered brief words of warning.

"If'n there's a argument comin' up that could turn rough, you watch that Carlin feller — you watch him, close! Because he packs a belly gun!"

Fraser showed a thin, mirthless smile. "Now that's mighty decent of you, Swede — telling me that. In return I'm buying you a drink. Come on — I want to look things over."

Quickly inside and behind the bar, Swede poured the drinks and watched Fraser anxiously. And thought he'd never seen such bleak, cold purpose on a man's face before.

"This 'un, Orde, is on the house," Swede murmured.

Fraser had his quick survey of the room, then put his drink away almost casually. But now, when he turned to face the room again, he was all fixed purpose.

Over at the poker table, Long Les Blackwell had come to his gangling full height, calling startled greeting. "Fraser! Never expected to meet you here. What's the idea? Maybe you wanted to see me about something?"

"Quite so," Fraser said, moving over to face Blackwell at close range. "First about the big double-cross. And I'm going to head it off!"

There had been some show of false joviality in Blackwell's first greeting. There was none at all in his next words.

"That's got a damn funny sound. What you driving at?"

"You know damn well what I'm driving at," Fraser lashed back. "The big steal, eh Blackwell? On my way from Humboldt City I did a lot of thinking, of adding up this and subtracting that, going over a lot of facts some very good friends of mine had put before me. And when I got through, there was just one answer. The big steal — the big double-cross! And it doesn't go, Blackwell. On my way out I also cut in a little toward the rim to see for myself what beef was feeding on this end of Rolling C range. And it is your stuff, Blackwell. It has no business there. So — get it off! All of it! And head it back where it came from!"

Lank and ungainly, Les Blackwell hunched his high shoulders forward. His hooded eyes pinched down and in their murky depths a fuming glow took place. His thin lips tightened into a pinched line and his whole appearance became one of cruel, predatory intent.

"You're crazy, Fraser," he droned. "That's fool's talk. Even if it was true, what authority you got to speak for Rolling C?"

"All I need," Fraser retorted. "I represent the owner of Rolling C — as the riding boss." Speaking, he gripped the edge of the table, leaning forward a little as though to add emphasis to his words.

All eyes in the room were on Fraser and Long Les Blackwell, all ears tuned for their words. So it was that no one noticed when the street door edged open and Starr Jennette slipped through.

Orde Fraser's flat statement of authority froze even Long Les Blackwell into momentary silence. Turk Roderick reared to his feet, drawing a deep, surprised breath. Then he measured Fraser with calculated, savage intent. Fitch Carlin leaned back in his chair, dropping both hands from sight below the table top.

Long Les Blackwell backed up a step before laying out his next words like a curse. "You're a fool, Fraser — a damned meddling fool! And I've only one answer for fools. All right, Fitch! . . ."

Listening and watching intently, every nerve in his body fine-drawn and alert, Orde Fraser saw Fitch Carlin's hands begin to lift. So he poured all his strength into a lifting shove that tipped the table, smashed it into Carlin, driving him and his chair back and over in a crashing fall.

Carlin had managed to get the muzzle of that belly gun just above the edge of the table, and now it pounded out in report, putting a bullet straight up through Swede Soderman's roof. Then Carlin was struggling wildly to get clear of the table and throw another and better-directed shot. But Fraser now had his gun stabbing out forward and down for a single shot. The slug hammered Fitch Carlin into a crumpled heap.

Now it was Turk Roderick who made his draw, his hating glance frozen on Orde Fraser. But before he could lift the muzzle of his gun level, another gun from behind Fraser smashed out its report. Turk Roderick grunted, spun half around and went limply down.

Fraser put his gun on Blackwell, then turned enough to locate the source of that last shot that had come only in time to head off Turk Roderick's deadly intended try at him. Starr Jennette was just sliding a reeking gun back into its holster.

"What you doing here?" Fraser demanded.

Starr Jennette's smile was slight and twisted. "Figured I might come in handy. Besides, I wanted to take a ride, so I could eat a lot of words along the way. I just swallowed the last of them. Then, too, I been looking for Roderick. I kinda wanted him special, seeing he tried to lay rough hands on a certain person you and I both know. I guess that tells it."

Some of the bleak wintriness drained out of Fraser's expression. "And it makes everything all right again, my good friend!"

He turned back to Lester Jason Blackwell and waved an indicating gun at the upset table and the two crumpled figures on the floor. "That enough authority for you?"

Blackwell stood as though stupefied, staring down at Fitch Carlin and Turk Roderick, two men who had lived by brutal violence and now had died because of it. In the hanging silence, Starr Jennette's soft but curt words were for the saddle hands at the bar.

"That's the way it goes, sometimes. Best leave it so!"

There was no argument about it. But presently Les Blackwell droned out what apparently to him was an incredible thought. "This — after I worked out a rich inheritance for you. My thanks for getting the Milliken Indian grant straightened out and made solid!"

Orde Fraser's laugh was bluntly skeptical. "Just so you could gobble it up later, after you had taken over Rolling C. Me and my inheritance were just handy chips in a case game. That was the real idea behind the whole thing, wasn't it? I think so. Don't try going holy on me now — it's too late for that. Frankly, you're lucky to be alive. But you won't stay that way unless, starting immediately, you begin moving every beef critter of yours off Rolling C range and head them back where they came from. Understood?"

Lester Jason Blackwell's glance had lost its arrogant glitter, was turning dull. "That will be done," he admitted. Then, because of the man's natural and never-failing avarice, he added, "I'd remind you of an advance I made, a matter of some two thousand dollars as I recall. What about that?"

239

"That money," Fraser said, "will be paid to Rolling C as a range fee for the grass your herd has already eaten. Don't try and press your luck, Blackwell. You're all through here."

High shoulder-points sagging, Long Les Blackwell turned and spoke an order to the saddle hands at the bar. "Get out with the stock. Tell Obie Steen that he's in charge and to start all our stuff back to the Owyhee immediately. Get at it!"

"A minute," Fraser said. "Carlin was your man, so you do the necessary with him. I'll send someone to do the same for Roderick. And now I guess that's about all." He turned to Jennette. "Don't know about you, Starr — but I could stand another drink."

He leaned against the bar, weary and drained. The fires that had driven him were burned out now, leaving only the cold and sour ashes of feelings gone flat and dead.

Jennette stood beside him. "Dan Larkin once said that all tigers walk softly. I know now what he meant."

"No tiger," denied Fraser gruffly. "Just a damn ordinary human being, and feeling like hell, now that it's over with. Swede, if you hadn't tipped me off about that belly gun, Carlin could have made his try good. The same goes for Turk Roderick if you hadn't bought in the way you did, Starr. So my big, big thanks to both of you!"

Swede shrugged. "You fellows are my kind of

people. Which makes me plumb happy."

Starr Jennette lifted his glass. "Never let the ghosts of what's over and done with hang around too long. Keep an eye open for the next sunrise. Get in on this one, Swede, because here's to better times ahead! . . ."

CHAPTER XIV

Orde Fraser slept that night at the Shoshone Lake line camp cabin, sharing all the news with Poe Darby and Andy Quider. From them he learned of Ike Britt's finish and from him they learned about Turk Roderick.

"Which just about cleans the slate," exulted unregenerate old Poe Darby. "Now folks can live decent and safe again!"

In the morning, Poe and Andy headed for Hayfork Crossing to do with Turk Roderick what they had done with Ike Britt. Fraser headed directly back to Humboldt City. At the stable, Benny Rust eyed him somewhat fearfully, but with enormous respect.

"This dun," Benny said, taking over the reins, "needs about a week of real rest. So should you do any more of this hellity-larrup travelin' around, you take a fresh bronc." About to turn away, Benny paused and added, "Starr Jennette came through last evenin', telling about affairs at Hayfork Crossing. Proves some of us were sure lookin' the wrong way at you. I was one of them. You can boot my pants for it, should you feel that way."

Fraser grinned slightly. "No need, Benny. We're still good friends."

Benny showed renewed spirit. "Nell Viney's got the fatted calf waiting for you at the hotel. Better go see."

One of the Indian girls was sweeping the hotel porch. The shy smile she showed Fraser was warm with welcome. The foyer was empty, but Nell Viney's call came down from the upper hallway.

"Bless you, boy! You've made me able to live with myself again. I'm not coming near you too soon or I'm apt to make a maudlin old fool of myself. You'll find Julie in the parlor."

This time she was standing and she turned to face him with a sort of restrained eagerness that carried with it a hint of wistful hesitancy as she spoke.

"Orde Fraser, I don't know what to say. I — I've been such a silly infant, and so wrong — so wrong. No — I just don't know what to say."

"That's easy," Fraser told her. "Just don't say it. Benny Rust tells me that Starr Jennette was in town last night with word of the Hayfork Crossing affair. So you know now that you will have no more trouble from Long Les Blackwell. It was a mean showdown, but history now, so I can bow out of the picture. I still say that Starr Jennette is one mighty good man and would make you a top hand riding boss."

Julie shook her head. "Starr and I talked that over again last night. We both know it wouldn't do. That is something that was settled a long time ago. By the fates, perhaps — if you believe in them. So there is just one person who is right for the job. That person is you, Orde Fraser."

"But my own ranch — what am I going to do with it? Girl, what's going on in that pretty head of yours? Look at me!"

He stepped close to her, put a finger under her chin and tipped her face so that her eyes were close to his own. Color surged up her throat, across the smooth, pure curves of her face, while her breathing became a quickened flutter. Her glance, though a little blindly, met and held his unwaveringly.

"It seems," he said gently, "that a man can never know when his trail is about to take a right-angled turn. Like how it is with you and me. I keep remembering how you looked that day in Iron Mountain, how when I passed by, admiring you, the look I got in return froze me to a crisp. Then there was how you faced me in this very room, vowing eternal enmity. Yet later that night you stepped into my room, a strange fear showing in your eyes — not fear of me, but of the strange way your life was working out. Particularly, I remember that night. Then there remains the exact moment and how you looked the first time you called me by my given name. And finally there was the way you looked at me in the bank, because that hurt me clear down to my heels. I'd rather you had shot me. Girl, when a man keeps remembering and treasuring such thoughts and moments, what does it mean — what does it mean? . . ."

Her eyes closed tightly, but still the tears squeezed through to bead her cheeks and leak down to a mouth that quivered, half-sobbing.

"For — for the way I acted in the bank, I've hated myself. For that I deserve nothing from you. But — oh, Orde — Orde! . . ." It ended in a little wail.

And somehow after that, magically enough, she was in his arms clinging to him. When later, she stepped back, her tear-washed eyes were starry.

"Girl," Fraser murmured, like a man bewildered — "How did this happen? . . ."

She laughed gaily. "Does it matter? Just so it did. Orde, let's go home? . . ."

"Home?"

"Rolling C, naturally. You can't manage a ranch without being there."

By the time they got away from town it was mid-afternoon. Several people watched them leave. Dan Larkin from the doorway of his office. Nell Viney from an upstairs hotel window. And Benny Rust, who saddled up for them. Viewers knew varied emotions, but Benny pretty well spoke for all of them when he murmured,

"Mighty pretty sight, watchin' them two ridin' off together. But it makes me feel kinda old and lonesome. . . ."

Much of the ride out to headquarters was made in silence, both of them held in the warm, close comfort of their thoughts. Presently, however, where the road swung close to the rim's towering flank, Julie reined in, exclaiming.

"Listen, Orde! . . ."

She stood in her stirrups, cupped her hands about her mouth and lifted a high, sweet call. The rim took the call and sent it back in echo, clear and true. Julie laughed her delight.

"Old rim never changes. Answers me just as it did back when I was a child, riding with my father."

Watching her, Orde Fraser again marveled at his fortune. Here was a woman grown, and in his eyes an ever increasingly lovely one, vital with charm and zest for living.

So they rode on, side by side, through a wide and beckoning land that was watched over and guarded by the great black rim.

By the rim that had always been there. The rim that would always be there. For the rim was time — and timeless!

The employees of Thorndike Press hope you have enjoyed this Large Print book. All our Thorndike and Wheeler Large Print titles are designed for easy reading, and all our books are made to last. Other Thorndike Press Large Print books are available at your library, through selected bookstores, or directly from us.

For information about titles, please call:

(800) 223-1244

or visit our Web site at:

www.gale.com/thorndike
www.gale.com/wheeler

To share your comments, please write:

Publisher
Thorndike Press
295 Kennedy Memorial Drive
Waterville, ME   04901